Until I Find Julian

Also by Patricia Reilly Giff

Until I Find Julian

patricia reilly giff

WENDY
LAMB
BOOKS

Visit us on the Web! randomhousekids.com

Educators and librarians, for a variety of teaching tools, visit us at RHTeachersLibrarians.com

Library of Congress Cataloging-in-Publication Data
Giff, Patricia Reilly.
    Until I find Julian / Patricia Reilly Giff.—First edition.
       pages   cm
    ISBN 978-0-385-74482-9 (hardback) — ISBN 978-0-385-74483-6 (lib. bdg.) — ISBN 978-0-385-74484-3 (ebook) [1. Missing persons—Fiction. 2. Brothers—Fiction. 3. Mexicans—United States—Fiction. 4. Illegal aliens—Fiction. 5. Emigration and immigration—Fiction] I. Title.
    PZ7.G3626Un   2015
    [Fic]—dc23
    2014046088

The text of this book is set in 13-point Adobe Caslon Pro.
Jacket design by Katrina Damkoehler
Interior design by Patrice Sheridan

Printed in the United States of America
10 9 8 7 6 5 4 3 2 1
First Edition

For my mother, Alice,
who said everyone has something
that is good and true,
for my husband, Jim,
who is everything good and true,
with gratitude for all these years
and deepest love,
and in memory
of George Nicholson,
editor, agent, mentor,
and beloved friend.

home

I'm in the worst trouble. How can I tell Mami and Abuelita what I've done?

I sneak along the alley and sit at the back of the house, leaning against the splintery boards, so angry with myself. I sweep up a pile of stones and toss them into the green creek, skipping them like frogs jumping from one slippery rock to another.

Sometimes the stones miss the water. My friend Damian says my aim is terrible. And he's right. With the next stone I hit a tree branch almost over my head, just missing my brother Julian's wooden birdhouses. Four or five finches fly up and scatter as a stray cat watches.

"Sorry," I whisper to the birds, and to the cat, who watches with great tawny eyes, ready to pounce on anything that moves.

I turn my head. Between the uneven boards of the house, I see Mama and Abuelita at the kitchen table, their heads bent over squares of cloth. They never stop working; they make scarves and quilts to sell at the market. Sometimes they sew red and yellow pieces together, or sunny greens and blues, reminding me of the creek.

They never stop talking either.

How can I go in there without any money?

Not one coin!

I close my eyes. Today, instead of sweeping at the car factory after school, Damian and I played catch with motor bolts while the foreman, Miguel, was eating in his office.

I missed, and the bolt flew over my head, denting a car door.

Damian slapped his head. "I should have known, Mateo."

Miguel came from his office, his mouth still full, pointing with his fist. "Out!" he yelled.

I couldn't stop laughing at first, thinking he was joking. But Miguel almost never joked or smiled. "Go on," he said, red-faced and furious. He didn't even pay me for last week's work.

Twelve years old, and I've been fired from my after-school job. A small job, but still . . .

Now I watch Mami and Abuelita stitching. I'll never be able to tell them!

I listen to what they're saying. It's the end of the month; my brother Julian will have sent money all the way from Arkansas. There'll be meat for dinner. Chicken, maybe, or small pieces of shredded beef mixed with rice and gravy.

Which will I pick? It doesn't do any good to tell myself I don't deserve a good dinner; my mouth waters. Chicken! I almost smell it stewing in the pot, with a pinch of one of Abuelita's spices that grow tall on the windowsill, and a carrot or two, chopped and soft.

"Enough to give you a handout," I whisper to the cat, and rest my hand on her grimy head.

The rap on the front door is loud. Someone is pounding hard; it must mean trouble. Mami stands up so suddenly the chair clatters and falls behind her.

I peer through the open spaces in the wall, to hear a voice calling. A moment later, Julian's old friend Tomàs fills the kitchen doorway.

Mami pushes a chair toward him. I can see the worry in her face. Why isn't Tomàs with Julian in Arkansas?

They crossed the border to work in America together. What's brought him back here?

Abuelita goes to the sink and pours a glass of water for Tomàs. He sits at the table facing them, slowly shaking his head.

I knot my fingers together, afraid to hear what he'll say.

When he speaks, his voice is low, his words slow and spaced apart. "Julian," he begins. "All of us. We worked on a building that would be the tallest one in town. Ten floors. Hard work. Satisfying."

"Please—" Mami says.

"Everyone knew we had no green cards." He looks up. "No permission to work in America. No permission even to be in that country."

Mami's hand covers her mouth as Tomàs tells of *la migra*, the border patrolmen, surrounding the construction area where they worked. "The illegal workers were loaded into the truck and sent to a detention center."

Abuelita sits straight, almost as if her back is made of iron. "And Julian?"

I hold my breath.

"We were on a scaffold, two flights up. Any minute they'd see us. I grabbed Julian's shoulder. 'We have to run. It's the only way.'

"I saw him peering over the edge.

"'No, Julian! We can't jump.'"

Tomàs puts a small roll of bills on the table. "Just before I backed off the scaffold, Julian reached into his pocket and asked me to bring this to you."

He spreads his hands wide. "The owner paid us good money. A generous boss. But now it's over. I don't know what my family will do for food."

Mami can hardly speak. "But Julian? Is he all right?"

"I don't know. I managed to climb down and run without being caught. But if he jumped, he may have been hurt. Maybe he's in prison. Or in hiding. I wish I could tell you more."

And what will we do? I lost my job with Miguel. Mami and Abuelita will have to sew long into the night.

I picture Julian just before he left: his hair was so dark it was almost black; his teeth were white and straight when he laughed. I looked up at his strong face. "Don't go! Stay! Mami said it's a dangerous trip. Thieves will take your money. And what about the desert, that huge river? What about the police on both sides of the border?"

He grinned and hugged me. "I've read so much about America—the mountains, the sea, the tall buildings. The prairie grass that waves in the wind." I could see the excitement in those dark eyes. "I want to be part of it, to paint all of it. I can't forget the money either. I'll work at anything and someday I'll find a place where I can draw, sketch—" He broke off. "In the meantime, I'll send money home. You know there are no jobs here."

He rested his hands on my shoulders. "This is the way I'll go. I'll walk miles to the train and climb on top . . ."

"You can't do that!"

He raised his hand. "After the train, I'll find some-one to take me across the north of Mexico and the river."

"You mean a coyote." I grabbed his collar. "Mami says they're desperate men. They rob the travelers, and sometimes they even kill."

"I'll be all right. Once I cross the border into Texas, I'll stop at our cousin Consuelo's house. And then, at last, Arkansas."

"But why Arkansas?" I ask.

"Tomàs says there's work up there. And I read about it. It sounds like a beautiful place."

Nothing I could say would stop him.

The next day he and Tomàs were on their way.

At the table now, Tomàs is still talking. "I have a long way to go. Home first. Then miles of walking to find a job. Any job at all."

Abuelita scrapes back her chair. I know she's going to pack what little food we have for his journey.

After Tomàs has gone, I still can't make myself go inside. I rest my hand on the cat, feeling the burning in my throat.

Mami bends her head over the squares as colorful as macaws, her tears dripping onto the fabric. Abuelita picks up her needle and begins to run stitches through two red pieces. Her eyes are almost closed. She won't let herself cry.

Julian has to be all right!

What will we do without the money he sends to the bank for us each month? Even worse, how will we know where he is, or how much trouble he's in? Letters hardly ever reach our town.

But we have to know.

I have to know.

I have to find him, save him, the way he saved me once.

And I know the way.

chapter 2

leaving

Tonight there's no chicken stewing in the pot, no shredded meat in our bowls. "It's been a long day." Abuelita tries to smile. "We'll have a little rice, a little bread instead."

I tell them about losing my job, but they hardly listen. Mami swipes a cloth over the counter in great arcs, her eyes swollen. She isn't speaking, she isn't singing. It's strange with no music in the kitchen. There's only the sound of the frogs croaking as they float on the water, their throats puffed into iridescent bubbles.

Mami doesn't want to tell me about Julian, not yet. I know she can't talk about it.

My little brother Lucas reaches out to me as if he knows something is wrong. I grab his hands and swing him around, just missing the table; he laughs, a smear of something across his cheek. The kitchen spins with us: the table with the bowls of rice, the wide window without glass, the green trees outdoors.

I put him down and sit at the table. I can't eat the rice in front of me. I'll do what Julian did: walk that long way to the train, then somehow cross the north of Mexico to the Rio Bravo. Texas is just on the other side of that river. Once there, I'll find Consuelo. I'm sure she'll tell me the rest of the way.

I take a forkful of rice. It has no taste; I'm not hungry even though I haven't had anything since breakfast.

My eyes go to Abuelita, the lines in her forehead deeper, then to Mami, staring out the window. She looks the way she did that terrible day Papi died. Our neighbors carried him home from the fields where he was planting in heat that soared over one hundred degrees. "His heart gave out," his friend Paulo told Mami. "The heat was too much for him."

Now, long after dinner, I go to bed and listen to the ripple of the creek and the faraway sound of a dog barking. I wait until the house is still.

The money I've saved to surprise Mami on her birthday goes into my pocket. I shrug into my old sweater and wrap a piece of cloth around my waist for a blanket.

Abuelita has left a new notebook for me in the kitchen closet. I copy Consuelo's and Julian's addresses from her pad, even though I'm sure I'll remember them.

I rest my hand on the notebook. Ah, Abuelita!

Once I told her, "I might write a book someday."

She nodded. "I know you will, Mateo. Everyone has something, and you have a way with words, *mi amor.*" In the kitchen, she cut paper into squares. With rough fingers, she stacked the pieces with a blue paper cover and stitched them together with string. She handed me the book, my first notebook. "Write down your memories: good ones and bad ones. Someday they'll turn into stories."

Now I slide two bottles of water and a few bits of food into my backpack. I tear a page out of the notebook and write quickly: *I've gone to find Julian.* I put it under Mami's breakfast plate. They won't find it until morning. Then I tuck the little book and a pen into my pocket.

I'm ready. I climb out the window and glance back at the sleeping house. Rain patters on the tin roof, and a mist rises up from the creek.

The cat is curled up under a tree. She'll have to hunt for every bit of her food from now on. I reach over and run my hands along her rough sides. Then I begin to walk.

Behind me, there's a voice.

I turn. Abuelita!

"You're going north across the border," she says.

I swallow. What can I say? "You found my note." I wonder if she'll tell me to go back inside.

She surprises me, though. "No, I haven't seen a note. But I knew you would go. I saw you outside listening when Tomàs was here." She touches my cheek. "It's a very dangerous trip. But I'd do the same thing if I were younger. We are alike, Mateo, you and I. We have great love for our family; it makes us strong."

We sit on the ledge next to the creek. "You must watch everyone and everything constantly." Her voice is stern. "Think before you act. Move slowly, carefully. Be deliberate."

Her eyes fill. I've never seen her cry, not even when Papi died. "You are everything to me." She slips a medal on a chain around my neck and money into my pocket. The medal matches the one she wears: Our Lady of Guadalupe.

"The lady, the Blessed Mother, appeared to a boy," Abuelita says. "She left her image and a spray of roses on his cloak. You can still see that cloak in Mexico City." She puts her hand on my shoulder. "She will protect you."

I watch her go back to the house, her head up. My tough Abuelita!

"I'll come back when I find him," I call after her.

And then I'm on my way.

chapter 3

the journey

I reach up to touch Abuelita's medal around my neck. It's been so long since she put it there. More than a week? It seems forever.

My eyes are closing as I listen to the sound of the motor and try to breathe inside the truck's close, dark air. I'm almost asleep.

Dreaming, Mateo. That's what it is.

I'm lost in dreams. I see our house that tilts against the creek, covered with Julian's paintings. It's miles behind me now. I hear Abuelita's husky voice as she reads to me.

Behind her, Lucas dances around the kitchen waiting for the beans to simmer in the enamel pot on the stove; his eyes are the color of walnuts and his hair grows every which way, just like mine. He sings a song he's just made up.

I feel Mami's floury hands on my cheeks.

And Julian: long ago, as I sleep in bed, creek water plinks on my cheeks; more slides down my neck. Green water, with the smell of weeds and fish! I reach up and grab Julian so he drops the cup, still half filled. We wrestle over the bed, onto the floor, laughing. He's eight years older than me, my best friend.

I'm in the back of a coyote's truck now; I concentrate on his red baseball hat, which stands out in this rusted heap as we try for the border.

In the beginning, I promised him money. "I'll pay you back someday."

He was chewing on something, ready to walk away, when he saw the watch on my wrist. Julian's watch. Too big for me, a little battered, but all I had left of him.

A moment later, the watch was off my arm, onto his. And I was crowded inside that truck with six others, holding my bare wrist.

Now the motor gives a dry cough. The truck heaves forward, then rattles to a stop. "We'll have to walk," the coyote says.

We stumble out and follow that red baseball hat.

I'm last. I can almost hear Damian saying, "Always last, Mateo. The cow's tail."

I wander into a thorny bush and fall over a hidden rock. "Ai!" Too far back for the coyote to hear. I've done something to one of my ribs. The pain is fierce. I lie there, holding my side.

My mouth is filled with grit; I've never been so thirsty. My face is sunburned, blistered, stinging more now that it's almost dark.

I want to cry like Lucas, to wail, to pound my fists.

Stop! Think about Mami and how frightened she is for Julian.

Think of Abuelita, who believes I can do this. I reach back to touch the little notebook in my jeans pocket. It's half filled now. I wrote in some of it after I left the train and waited to find a coyote, and a few pages more as I crouched in the back of that smoky truck.

I've told about my journey: the days of walking and sleeping near the road, then racing along next to the train heading north, hauling myself up, the train speeding around curves, the wind and bits of debris so strong I couldn't open my eyes. My feet sliding, my legs . . .

I held on to the railing as my sweater flew off my shoulders, the scrap of blanket was ripped off my waist, and the backpack hurtled away.

But I wrote about happier things too: Lucas loving music, waking us with his songs. And our house, which

Abuelita and my long-ago Abuelo built with their own hands.

"We worked at the factory until we could buy nails," Abuelita told me. "We'd picked up boards that floated down the green creek."

She held out her hand to show me her crooked fingers. "From raising the roof." Still she smiled. "We loved doing it."

They painted the house blue, but not just an ordinary blue. It was the color of a bluebird's wing, the color of the sky on a hot summer morning.

Julian's favorite color.

Later, Julian drew pictures of all of us on the walls. He stood on the table in the kitchen, his head grazing the ceiling, and painted wrens flying in and out of birdhouses, just the way they did outside. And while he worked, he tossed English words to me over his shoulder. *"Broom,"* he'd say. "You use it to sweep for Abuelita. Weed the vegetables. You do that too." He grinned. "Not often enough."

How did people speak such a hard language?

But Julian wouldn't give up. Every day a new word!

I move now and feel a quick pain in my side.

Ahead, the coyote yells at a woman who's fallen behind. "Leave the baby," he shouts, "or I'll leave you here and you'll both die."

I watch, terrified. What will she do? What can she

do? But the woman struggles on, and the coyote turns, paying attention to someone else.

I scramble to my feet, holding my side.

The coyote stops, his arm raised, standing completely still.

I hear it too.

The rumble of a motor growing louder.

Lights flashing through the yucca trees. It's a truck coming fast, too fast for me to think, to run.

Who could it be? Police? Or even worse: thieves, looking for money?

The coyote, baseball hat gone, dives behind a jumble of rocks; the others scatter like ants, dropping bags, the baby wailing as the truck swerves toward them.

The lights sweep over me. I drop down and dig myself into the ground, my heart beating so fast I can hardly breathe, my mouth open, sand on my teeth, on my tongue. I don't dare to whisper, but I think: *Don't see me. Don't . . .*

The travelers disappear behind rocks, behind scrub bushes. It's as if they don't exist. Even the baby is silent. The truck idles; two men in front lean forward, searching for them. But it's no use. After a few moments, they turn the truck and disappear too.

Nothing is left but paper bags filled with fruit and bottles of soda, or water, hot from the day's fierce sun, a few pieces of clothing, a baby's blanket, all scattered across the ground.

The coyote, a shadow, head down, comes from behind the bushes and heads back the way we've come. He just misses me. I turn slowly and watch after him, listening as he whistles to himself.

I crouch there, afraid to move. Suppose the men in the truck come back?

And then I realize I'm alone. Not one of the travelers returns for his things. I'm really alone.

Sounds surround me: wind, beating insect wings. A lizard darts away, its feet and curved tail leaving delicate traces behind it.

Everything is suddenly still: the small creatures, and even the wind. It's as if the earth knows I'll never find my way to the river that flows along the border. I'll never find Julian in the north.

All the stories I've heard about people crossing the border come flooding into my head. Mami, when she was twenty, hoping for a job, was lost for hours, and then caught and sent home. Mr. Juarez, who'd lived across the creek from our house, was killed by coyotes for a few pesos. A boy from our village was turned away from the border four times, and finally gave up.

I raise my head, remembering the bags left by the travelers. I can't wait to taste the fruit, to feel its sweetness sliding down my throat that's as dry as the desert sand.

And bread! I'll bite off huge chunks and eat until I'm full. Maybe I'll find another sweater and that poor baby's blanket for the cold nights.

What would Mami say? How terrible to be glad I'd have what the poor people left. But I am glad, my thirst is terrible, and in another moment I'll have something to drink.

I crawl forward slowly, my side aching, and hear something.

What?

A large animal?

I cover my head with my hands.

It's not an animal. It's the sound of feet.

If only Julian were still at home with us.

If only I were home, writing in my book, the stray cat curled up next to me, the sound of the creek out back, water lapping against the rocks.

chapter 4

caught

Someone is right behind me, coming fast.

If I get hurt I'll be no help to Mami and Abuelita, no help to Lucas. And I'll never find Julian!

A foot digs hard into my back, pushing me down. I spit out a mouthful of earth.

Someone breathes over me. "Move," the voice mutters.

I slide out from under the foot slowly, dirt scratching the side of my face and my arms. "Don't." I try to sound hard, to sound tough.

"Pathetic." There's something strange about that high voice.

I peer up over my shoulder.

A girl stares at me, her hand to her mouth!

Her face is filthy. Her jeans are in tatters, the hems in strings. Her ragged shirt is stained, and one sleeve is gone.

Her hair hasn't been combed in weeks; maybe it's never been combed. It hangs in thick ringlets down her back—probably dark, but dirt covers it, so it looks almost gray, even though she must be about twelve years old, my age.

I stand, wiping my face, then my shirt, trying not to groan as I feel the pain in my side. I look up at her; she's tall and gawky like a stork. Her sharp elbows stick out as she rests her skinny hands on her hips.

She grins. "It's a wonder you've lasted out here as long as you have, bumping into things, yelling at a little fall. Probably crying like a baby."

"Wrong," I say, in a voice that matches hers.

"You're looking for the river," she says. "A hard place to cross, impossible if you can't swim."

"I can swim." My voice is hoarse; I'm so thirsty and my tongue is so thick I can hardly get the words out.

I have a quick thought of that soupy creek in back of our house: shallow, cool, not wide enough to take more than a few strokes. A place to dip my face. A place to stand with Julian to hook a fish for dinner.

She tells me about a horrible death by drowning in that river: choking, both feet tangled in reeds, eyes sealed shut in mud.

This girl is trying to scare me. She's doing a good job! I can't let her know that, though.

I take a step away from her, and then I'm almost running toward the bags the immigrants left: the water, an orange half-hidden in the sand.

I sink down, the girl almost forgotten, and twist off the top of a bottle. With my head back, I drink until I can't hold any more.

She's next to me now. She picks up a canvas bag, empties it in the sand, and picks through everything, dropping pieces of fruit and bread back into the bag, a bottle of water, then takes time to roll a small blanket tightly so it fits on top.

She wraps a sweater around her neck and glances at me as she tears the rind off the orange with her teeth. She sucks on the fruit, her nose turned up. "If I'm going to save your life, I should probably know your name."

"Mateo." I stare at her. "Why would you help me? You don't even know me."

She runs her tongue over her lips, which are caked with sand, hesitating, staring again. "No time for that now." She shoves her hair off her face. "Call yourself Matty. At least try to sound as if you come from the north." She spreads her arms. "I'm Angel. A guardian angel, like Gabriel or Raphael in the Bible. I'm just missing the wings."

She pokes out her hand.

Angel the stork, I think. We shake hands. Crazy thing to do in the desert.

She doesn't wait for me. She slings the bag over her shoulder and begins to walk. "I know this place better than anyone," she calls back. "I know the washes; I've seen where the rattlers and scorpions nest; I know where the tall yuccas are and the plants with thorns that tear your skin."

She stops. "I left my grandfather's house. I've crossed over many times. It gives me something to do."

She's quiet then, moving fast now, feet slapping, the bag swinging.

I can't lose her; I scoop up a bag. I don't even know what's in it. I follow a few steps behind, holding my side with one hand.

It's long after dark when she stops again. "Smell that?"

My nose is clogged with sand. How can I smell anything? Now that she's just standing there, I crouch down to rest and pull off my sneakers slowly. My feet are blistered, bleeding; one toenail is hanging.

"A mistake," she says. "You probably won't be able to get them on again."

"I know what I'm doing." I hear the anger in my voice even though I know she's right.

She ignores my feet and my temper. "I can smell the river ahead of us. After you cross that, you'll be a wetback."

Wetback. Wet from the river. I've heard that American word before. Miguel at the factory calls Julian that. Not a nice word coming from Miguel's mouth.

She's pointing now, and it's there, almost like a miracle: a wide swath of river swirling around a small island in the center. The water's dark and a little muddy, almost like the creek in front of our house.

"We'll cross later on," Angel says. "If you can't swim, if you're lying, you'll drown."

She knows I'm lying, but still my head goes down. It's been so long since I've slept. I need five minutes. Ten.

I close my eyes.

"And if you sleep, they'll catch you, throw you in prison for who knows how long, then send you back wherever you belong."

My eyes fly open. "I'm not sleeping." I look away from her, embarrassed. "I can swim . . . a little."

"I knew it." She bites her lip. "We'll have to use an inner tire tube I've hidden away. I pump it up once in a while. I hope it isn't poked out with holes now. I don't have time to babysit you. I have things to do." She hesitates. "This is the most dangerous part." She points across the river with one hand; her nails are rimmed with black.

I stand searching. I don't see anything, but to have come all this way for nothing!

Angel yanks the edge of my shirt, pulling hard so I move into the shelter of a knob of trees. "You're just dying to be caught."

My face is inches from hers. "I've traveled a long way alone. I can even cross this river without you."

"You don't know what you're talking about," she says.

I take a breath. Mami said that a long time ago. And I'm reminded of something else: a froth of water, rocks, a sheer drop, the far end of the creek at home.

She rolls a stone in her mouth and acts as if we haven't been whispering furiously at each other. "We'll wait until it's dark again. Until, just for a moment, *la migra* needs coffee, or changes shifts, or travels somewhere else, and then we move."

I reach in my pocket for the pen and the small notebook. There are hours to wait, hours to write down my memories.

I Remember . . .

It wasn't my turn to weed the rows of vegetables on the side of the house. "The weeds don't harm anything anyway," I told Mami.

"You don't know what you're talking about," she said. "Go and weed, Mateo. Do you want to eat the vegetables when they're ripe? Do you even want to have dinner? It's suppertime soon, you know."

I didn't want dinner. Who'd want rice boiling on the stove when the whole world was boiling hot? "I'm six years old," I said. "Old enough to run away."

"Goodbye," Mami said.

"I'll miss you, Mateo," Abuelita said.

Lucas waved at me.

"When Julian comes home from work, tell him I'll see him one day," I said over my shoulder.

I went out the door, held open with a brick to catch a breeze that might come our way. A few steps and I reached the creek. The green water was shallow from the dry summer weather; it was deeper far down when it reached the rocks and fell over into a pool.

Yes, a perfect spot for me. I'd wade in the pool, eat plums from the trees heavy with fruit. I'd sleep on the soft grass with the song of the frogs to keep me company.

I'd never weed the vegetables again.

Barefoot, I walked along the edge of the creek. It was a long way, almost forever, it seemed. Head down, I passed the old woman's house on the other side of the water. I didn't need her yelling at me.

I went faster when I heard the sound of the water running over the rocks, loud enough to drown out the sound of the frogs. I was close to my new home.

I sank down to catch my breath. Mami would be sad by now, sorry her middle son had run away forever. And what about Abuelita? I knew I was her favorite, even though she'd never said so. I could tell by the way she put her hand on my head, the way she gave me an extra scoop of rice.

Poor Abuelita.

And what about me? No mother, no abuelita, no brother Lucas, and most of all, no brother Julian.

"Don't feel sorry for yourself," I muttered. I wiped my head that was wet from the heat. It was time to swim in the pond under the falling water.

I climbed up the slippery rocks that Mami had warned me about once; my toes gripped them so I wouldn't fall and be gone forever.

And I didn't fall; I didn't even stumble. I was across the rocks in a few moments.

See, I told myself. *Don't worry, I can do anything.*

I lay on one of the rocks and looked at the water below. It rushed along in a great froth of white, tumbling over on itself, then flattening out at the far end, where it seemed calm, a perfect place to swim, to float along, the heat seeping out of my body.

But I had to get there.

How would I do that?

I imagined myself standing at the very edge of the rock, arms raised, flying, diving high over the water, then rushing along with that white froth, until I reached the calm part, where I could hear the frogs again.

What a brave thing to do.

I held my nose so I wouldn't be flooded with water, counted to seventy.

It was as far as I could count. . . .

And jumped.

I hardly felt the air rush along, the water coming up and up. I was tumbling, turning, water roaring, filling my mouth and burning my nose. I couldn't stand, couldn't swim, couldn't yell for help. . . .

Couldn't . . .

Breathe.

But then something dragged me out of the water.

What? Who?

I lay on the grass, coughing, sneezing, taking huge breaths, feeling Julian's hand on my back. "You're all right, Mateo," he kept saying. "I have you. Cough! Give back the water."

And then I really was all right.

I sat up, leaning against him. "You saved me."

He grinned at me. "You needed saving."

"Nobody else cared."

"Oh, they cared. I came home just after you left. They sent me after you. Mami and Abuelita are waiting at the edge of the creek."

The warmth of that spread through my chest, but Julian wasn't finished. "They want you to know they'll be glad to have you back." He was laughing now. "After all, they need someone to weed the vegetables."

"I guess I could do that."

"What you did was dangerous. What would we do without you, Mateo?"

My throat was still burning. "You're the best, Julian. I'll save you sometime too. I promise."

Julian stood and pulled me to my feet. "I know you will."

We walked home together. I was hungry now, starving. I couldn't wait for a bowl of rice.

chapter 5

the river

Still half asleep, I open my eyes, mumbling, "I'll find you, Julian."

"Who's Julian?" Angel asks.

I stumble through the story: *My brother gone, Arkansas, the unfinished building.* She watches me, not saying a word.

The heat of the day has melted into a cooling breeze that soothes my sunburned face and arms. The pain in my side is melting away, too.

At last it's dark. Angel shoves the inner tube along

the river's edge and guides me into the water with her hand on my back.

I tie my sneakers together by their strings, hang them around my neck, and maneuver myself into the tube, my feet still gripping the sandy bottom. The tube is slippery and water soaks my shirt and jeans.

"Go," Angel whispers.

Courage, Abuelita would say. I feel her small silver medal around my neck. Will it protect me?

Droplets bubble up from a small slit in the rubber, and I cover the leak with the palm of my hand. *This will be the end of me. They'll find me, feet tangled in the reeds, eyes covered with mud, choking.*

"Move." Angel sounds impatient that I still stand there, the tube like a huge bracelet around my waist.

I let go with my feet, and the sneakers slung around my neck fill with water.

"No noise," she whispers fiercely. "No splashing."

I kick against the fast-moving water, my legs deep under the surface. Head up like a turtle, I keep my eyes on the island in the center of the river.

Crossing this wide river takes forever. Halfway to the island, I rest my cheek against the tube, and even though I can't see Angel, or hear her, she must be only a few feet behind me.

And she was right again. I never would have been

able to swim across this river; I never would have made it by myself.

But is she really there?

Maybe not.

Keep going.

She might be back on the bank, grinning as I flounder around in the river. I don't know anything about her. When I told her about Julian, why didn't she tell me why she's here? Why she's helping me?

I turn my head, hoping to catch a glimpse of her, or at least to hear her. Then I see those skinny arms slipping silently in and out of the water behind me. One hand reaches out and pushes the tube.

I hear the soft ripple of tiny waves against a row of stones ahead of me. My feet feel the sand again, and my toes slide along the gritty bottom.

The trees reach out to me from this small island, thin wispy trunks in the darkness, and leaves rustle the way they do at the edge of the creek at home.

I drag myself out of the river, dripping wet and so cold my teeth chatter. I pull the slippery tube along; my blistered feet dig into the stony ground. But the north is just yards away, across this side of the river, about the distance from our house to the turning of the creek at the edge of town.

I can do the rest.

I know I can.

Without thinking, feeling joy that I've conquered the desert and most of the river, I call, "I'm coming, Jul—"

I never finish. Angel's sandy hand covers my mouth so hard that my teeth bite into my lips.

I bat her hand away. "What's the matter with you?" I wipe the sand off my mouth with a quick motion, letting her know how annoyed I am.

"It would be just my luck to save a helpless thing like you," she whispers, her face an inch away from mine. "And be caught myself with your noise."

"Get lost," I say.

She sinks down against a tree and pulls me with her.

My chin juts out. "You're making just as much noise."

She roots around for a stone. Head back, she drops it in her mouth, sucking on it. I can hear it grate against her teeth.

Something swims along nearby, a beaver maybe, with a white curve of water behind it.

I look up. One side of the river belongs to my country; the other side belongs to the north. How high in the sky is it before the world doesn't belong to anyone . . . or maybe belongs to everyone?

A cloud moves slowly across the sky, covering it for a moment. It floats over to our side, to our country. For a while the cloud should belong to me, and Abuelita, and Mami.

Angel snaps her fingers. "Pay attention, Matty."

We push off again. The inner tube rubs against my skin; water slaps against my sunburned face and arms. Angel swims ahead. The wake she leaves is no wider than the beaver's.

Across the way, I bump to a stop. This is *el norte*, the United States.

A small hill rises in front of me, cutting off what's beyond. Men with guns? A police station? Who knows?

Angel and I crawl to the top of the hill and peer over the edge. There's nothing but a few trees, bent and weird, with belongings scattered among them. We scuttle around like a pair of crabs, heads down, to see what we can find to take with us.

Angel picks through one bag; she finds a cocoa-colored sweater that almost matches her eyes. There's no food, and nothing to drink. But I spot a wooden handle sticking out of a bag; it's the same color as the sweater Angel has tossed around her neck.

I dust off sand and grit, and zip open the bag. Inside is a musical instrument. I ease it out.

"A guitar," Angel says.

Yes, a guitar.

The strings are loose, lying there on top like the small waves we sometimes see in the creek at home. I run my hands over each one, but there's no sound.

The strings should be tight.

I fiddle with the keys, if that's what they're called,

turning the knobs one at a time. Each string begins to tighten; the waves disappear.

I pluck one of them, and . . .

I hear Mami singing in the kitchen. Abuelita stirs a pot on the stove, and Lucas drums his fingers against the wooden table, loving music as much as Mami.

Lucas could probably play this guitar.

Julian, Lucas, and I used to camp out near the creek when it was too hot to sleep indoors. And one night, a wind came up. "Listen," Julian said. "The trees with their branches waving sound like music."

Lucas tilted his head, nodding.

I pluck another string and imagine the music Lucas would make.

Angel pushes my arm. "Stop," she whispers. "Someone will hear you."

I brush my fingers over the strings, then slide the guitar back into its canvas case and loop the strap over my shoulder.

"What are you doing?" she asks.

I feel as if I'm holding on to my family. I can't tell her that, though. She'd think I was crazy. I can't tell anyone, except maybe Lucas. I'll bring this guitar home to him and put it in his hands.

"Let's go before we're caught." Angel brushes the dust off the sweater.

"I'm ready," I tell her, and I am.

chapter 6

samson, texas

I reach into my pocket, feeling for the small notebook and the addresses. It's soaked from the river! It's still dark, but in the moonlight, I can see that the book is ruined, water-soaked. I can't read one word, not one number.

I'd pictured showing a book of memories to Julian. He'd listen, head bent, smiling a little as he remembered saving me from the creek.

It's lucky I remember both addresses. Julian's is strange, with lots of numbers; the cousin's is almost as long. At home, we have only one: Six Creek Road, even though there really isn't a road. It's a dirt path with overhanging trees, and sometimes a small green snake or two, friendly guys who doze along the branches.

Angel and I crawl into some of the undergrowth to try to sleep for a while. I lie still, wary of thorns. For the thousandth time I ask myself, What happened to Julian? Was he hurt? Caught by the police? Is he in prison?

Stop!

I close my eyes, but I jump at every sound, even the scuttle of insects as they click by.

What if I hear a truck, or heavy footsteps coming closer with rough hands clamping down on my shoulders?

And then, just as I imagined it, a hand grips my arm. But it's Angel's. "Wake up, Matty. We have to leave soon."

A pink sky lights the early morning. Angel wanders over to a bubbling stream that comes out of the rocks and scoops handfuls of water over her face. She ducks her head so the ends of her hair float like small fish, then quickly dunks her head four or five times. When she comes back, there's a clean round spot on each cheek and her pointy nose is covered with freckles; her hair is lighter and shiny. She sinks down against the tree. "What will you do next?"

"I have a plan." Not so helpless after all. "My cousin lives in Samson. I'll stop there first. Maybe she can help me get across Texas into Arkansas."

Angel holds up her hand, palm toward me. "I might as well hang around for a while and see what happens." She glances up at the sky, considering. "Yes, I guess so."

I shrug. "Why not?"

"Where is this house?" She's sucking on a stone again.

I hesitate. "I've never been there. They have a farm. Abuelita told me once that it's on top of a hill, but it looks as if it might slide off any minute."

Angel slaps her forehead. "Impossible. There must be dozens of places like that."

"I remember the address."

"All right. We'll ask someone who looks friendly."

I drag myself to my feet. The sun glows over the horizon now, turning broad leaves green, and earth the color of rich brown silk.

It's going to be another hot day, but I don't mind. My clothes are damp; they need to dry. And I'm cold, trying not to shiver, my arms crossed over my chest.

We walk forever, and the sun beats down now. My shirt has dried; my hair is plastered to my head; my feet burn. I fall behind Angel, thinking of water and standing in the cool creek.

She glances back. "What's the matter with you? It's that guitar—too heavy, probably waterlogged."

"Not the guitar." I take big steps, almost the way Lucas would, showing her I can keep up, that I can walk even faster than she can.

She waves both arms at a van that's coming slowly along the middle of the road, tailpipe clanking. "Wait, please," she calls.

The van rumbles to a stop. We run toward it so Angel can ask the driver for directions.

The driver is a woman with a sunburned face and frizzy hair. "It's a long way," she says in my own language. "Miles." She must see how tired we are. "I'll give you a lift."

We climb in and bump along, listening to the woman singing. Angel and I stare at each other. We never would have walked this in a day.

At last the woman points with her thumb.

And yes, there's a dirt road almost like the one at home; it circles up a hill.

"Thanks," I call after her.

We climb the hill, passing falling-down houses and trees that line the road.

We see Consuelo's farm. The mailbox by the road is missing its lid, but it has the right address painted on one side. The house is old; the unpainted boards are silver gray. Chickens wander around in the yard, clucking and pecking at tufts of grass, and at each other.

A guy comes around to the front, carrying wooden boxes on his shoulder. He's older than Julian but looks a little like him. He stops when he sees us and puts the boxes on the ground. "Hey," he says.

"I'm Mateo," I tell him. "My cousin Consuelo—"

"You're family, then," he cuts in. "From across the border."

I nod. "Consuelo—"

"My mother, but she's not here. Sorry." He raises one shoulder. "She's gone visiting, back in a week or so."

He must see the disappointment on my face. He grins. "I can manage something to drink, though. Maybe some breakfast."

Before I can answer, Angel is saying yes, breakfast would be great. Sometimes she's really annoying.

Inside the house, we sit at the kitchen table while the cousin, Felipe, warms tortillas and fries eggs for us. He listens as I tell him we're on our way to Downsville, Arkansas.

"Where your brother lives," he says.

I nod. It's too much to tell him about Julian, and I have no time anyway. He slides the eggs onto our plates and says, "You're in luck if you don't mind riding along with boxes of fabric that I'm going to sell."

He slides onto a chair, grinning with overlapping teeth. "I'm on my way. Not exactly to Downsville, but close enough. There's room in the back, if you want to go along."

"Yes." I can hardly speak, I'm so relieved.

Felipe nods toward the screen door. "The dog sits in front."

A mangy-looking dog with yellow fur and a thumping tail stares in at us. I grin at Felipe.

I'm starving. I shovel in the eggs, take huge bites of the tortilla, which drips melted butter, and wash it all down with bitter black coffee that Felipe pours from a metal pot.

On the counter is a thick pad. "Could I take a piece of paper?" I ask. "And that pen?"

"Sure. Take the whole thing." He waves his hand, and I slip them into my pocket. The pages are wrinkled, and someone has doodled over a few, but I can't wait to write.

We spend the next hour loading the truck with boxes. "Glad you came along," Felipe says.

We climb in and settle against the rough side boards.

Angel grins. She's half asleep, her voice thick. "A long way."

I lean forward. "Why are you coming with me?"

"Nothing else to do right now," she mumbles.

A strange girl!

Before I can say anything, her head drops; her eyes are closed. "Diego?" I think she whispers, but she's asleep.

What can I tell her about Julian?

What can I write about him?

I pull the pad out of my pocket and begin.

I Remember . . .

A day, just like today, sunny and hot, too nice for school. I sneaked out of the house with my fishing pole over my shoulder, slid down along the mud next to the creek, and sat against a tree, heart pounding.

What would Mami think about my skipping school? What would Abuelita say?

I didn't worry for long, though.

Fishing in the creek would be better than the math review we were having that day. And maybe with forty kids in the class, my teacher might not notice I was missing.

I could see a fish, but it saw me too in the reflection of

the water: my every-which-way hair that I hadn't combed, my ears that stuck out a little from my head, my skinny arm holding the pole. With a flick of its silver tail, the fish was gone, over to the other side of the creek to rest in the shade of an overhanging tree.

I didn't care.

But then I heard Julian singing, his voice loud as he came along the side of the creek. It was something about a frog that waited to snap up a fly, one of Lucas's songs. He was on his way home to sleep after a night working for Miguel at the factory.

I hadn't thought of Julian. What would he say when he saw me fishing in my school pants, which I saw now were muddy?

Before I could dart away like the silver fish, there was Julian's reflection in the still water. He stopped in the middle of the song and I hunched my shoulders.

But he didn't say what I thought he might.

"Saw a frog," he began to sing again. And I sang too.

We finished the song and he kept going.

I stayed there, the song in my head, fishing, until I was sure school was over and I could go home again.

Ah, Julian. He never told on me.

But a week later, a painting hung over my bed. It was me, fishing, my head back, eyes closed. My pants were rolled up and muddy. But only Julian and I knew they were my school pants. We both grinned when we looked at it together.

chapter 7

the house

It's more than hours. It's forever. The next day, until late afternoon. We eat the sandwiches Felipe has put together. Sometimes we hear him slow down and stop; then he talks to people, but we huddle between boxes. We sleep. We wake. Then, at last, he lets us off near Julian's house. "Straight along that road," he says. "I'd take you the rest of the way, but I'm late."

We stumble out of the truck; the sun is sinking on the far edge of the horizon.

Felipe gets out too. We hug and thank him; we promise to stop and see him on the way home.

"Don't forget," he calls as he slides back into his seat. We wave goodbye as he pulls away.

"I'll tell my mother—" he calls back, but the rest of his words are lost with the roar of the truck.

We march along the road, faster now, almost there! At the top of the street we stop to stare at a big house with shiny glass windows. It's painted white with a line of cactus plants throwing their crooked arms up to the sky. The house is even larger than the one that belongs to Miguel, the factory foreman who fired me at home.

"Whew," Angel says. "A rich guy."

Julian? No. As I count the numbers on the door, I see that it's not Julian's place. Of course not. "I wrote about him while we were in the truck," I tell her. "You can read it later."

She twitches one shoulder. "What is he doing here, anyway? Making money?"

"He's not here anymore. At least, I don't think so. This is just where he was."

I walk up the street, searching. "If I had enough money," he said once, "I'd put up a little house in *el norte*, or maybe even a tent. I'd farm a bit, and draw foxes at night, and the birds and geese during the day."

And there's his house, in the middle of a row of houses; most of them seem empty. They're attached and lined up the way Lucas lines his toy blocks along the floor. The roofs are flat. You could run on top of those houses from one end of the street to the other.

Julian's house doesn't look friendly the way ours does at home. Charcoal paint has chipped off in spots, showing paler gray underneath; the front steps list to one side. And the square bit of grass in front is brown in spots. But it isn't that. Maybe it's the windows with the faded curtains that hide the inside from the street.

I shiver. Who'd want to live here?

I think of our house, the stray cat curious, her sharp claws reaching through the cracks in the boards, the sun drawing square patterns of light across the bedroom floor and the kitchen wall.

Please let Julian still be here in this terrible house, waiting for me.

I dream about what could happen next. I'd bang hard on the door. As he pulled it open, he'd mutter, "Who's making all that noise?" and I'd be standing there.

Angel taps my shoulder with her fingers. "I guess I'll leave you here."

In the middle of nowhere?

"So long, Matty." She takes a few steps away. She doesn't look like her usual take-charge-of-the-world self.

"Where are you going?"

She raises one bony shoulder. "Anywhere." She keeps

going, walking faster, swinging her arms, as if she's forgotten all about me.

"Angel?" My voice is loud, almost as bossy as hers.

She doesn't turn, but she stops, her hands on her hips, her sharp elbows out like a pair of triangles.

"Want to hang out for a while?"

She doesn't answer.

"Help me find my brother?"

"You can't do that alone?"

I open my mouth, ready to say *get lost,* but her voice sounds strange, garbled, almost as if she's trying to hold back tears. She's all alone. Maybe she needs a friend. Maybe that's why she was so willing to help me.

"I guess I can't," I make myself say.

"All right, then." She walks toward me, sneaker laces flapping. "I'll stay, but only for a couple of days. I have a bunch of things to do. Do you think I can waste my whole life with you?"

"No," I say. I see she's trying not to smile. I see how happy she is. So I'm right about her being lonely. And then I remember hearing her whisper a name in the truck. What was it? Dario? Desiderio? "Who's . . . Danilo?" I ask.

"How should I know?" She wipes her hands on the sides of her jeans. "Let's go," she says, back to her bossy self. "Do you want to stand here forever?"

I take a breath and go up the cracked cement path to the middle house. The bell is broken. I knock a few times, then turn the handle, but the door doesn't budge; it's locked, of course. I listen, but inside, everything is still. I stand on tiptoes to peer through the window on top.

The living room, if that's what it is, is almost empty: no rug, no chairs; only a couch, a table full of scratches, and a TV.

A TV! We don't have one at home. We don't have an iPhone or an iPad, or any of those things I hear about in school.

"Someday," Mami said, sighing.

Angel doesn't wait for me. "We'll go around the back," she calls over her shoulder. She cuts across the weedy lawn and disappears along the side of the house.

She's impossible.

I follow her, though. What else is there to do?

There's one backyard for all the houses. It's filled with junk: an old tire, pieces of wood, a table turned upside down. Four brightly colored wooden birdhouses hang from a tree. They match the birdhouses that hang over our door. Julian!

I circle around to the steps and glance up to see a fuzz of green trees in the distance.

Angel is in the kitchen, her hand on the faucet; rusty water runs in the sink. She shrugs. "The door wasn't even locked."

She motions to me, still on the step. "Move it, Matty. We don't want the whole world to see we've broken in."

I shake my head. "We didn't break in," I say as I go inside. "It's Julian's place." *Was* Julian's place? "Besides, it was your idea, Angel."

The water runs clear in the sink now, and Angel takes a sip.

How strange. There's nothing in this kitchen of Julian's that I recognize. "Almost empty," I whisper. There's a smell of sour milk.

"Not exactly. We haven't looked in the cabinets yet. And there's an old cup in the sink. A plate, a spoon, a bowl of half-eaten cereal, and a half-eaten piece of toast on the counter."

I nod. The cup in the sink is half filled with dried-out coffee. *"I can't start the day without it,"* Julian said.

"Your brother isn't going to win any prizes for keeping a neat house," Angel says, and hesitates. "Maybe he left in a hurry."

How can I tell her about Julian? That he's usually neat, that he's a terrific cook, and when he talks, he always has his hand on someone's shoulder.

Outside, someone is walking a dog. Angel looks up. A flash of unease crosses her face. She puts her finger to her lips and runs out of the room.

We're far from the border now. We don't look as if we belong. And we certainly don't belong in this house.

I stand back, peering out the window to see a woman on the sidewalk. As I turn to follow Angel, my arm grazes the bowl on the counter. It tilts, spins! I reach out, too late, as it smashes on the floor.

I'm frozen, listening. Outside, the footsteps stop. Maybe I should open the door and tell her who I am, ask if she's seen Julian. But I don't know that many words in English. It won't help to say: *The cat is scrawny.*

Scrawny. I love the feel of that in my mouth.

And what about *Clouds are puffy?*

Puffy, a good word too.

Julian taught me those.

I try to remember what I know, and begin to whisper to myself: the days of the week, *broom* and *sweep, fish after work.* What else?

But suppose the woman outside calls the police?

Another word: *illegal.*

I can't take a chance.

I skirt around the broken bowl and the lumps of cereal and dive into the bedroom behind Angel, closing the door. I check to be sure the long curtains cover the window in case the woman peers in.

A clock with a dusty face stands on a small table; the hands have stopped at twelve. When I pick it up the battery falls out: the whole thing's a mess. Was it even Julian's?

I look out the window. The woman is gone. I sink

down on the edge of the bed. The closet door is half open, and there are clothes inside. Julian's clothes? A pair of jeans, the hems in strings, and a pair of sneakers as worn as mine, with rubber missing at the toes.

I turn. On the bed is a patchwork quilt made with red and yellow squares. It lights up the room, even though it's a little torn, a little dirty. It's come a long way. I flip it over, and in neat dark stitches, I see the initials, Mami's and Abuelita's.

I run my hand over it, patting it, almost the way I'd pat the cat's head. If only I could find Julian. I'd fly home like one of Julian's birds and be there in time for dinner.

"What's going on with you?" Angel bangs her hand on the door molding.

She sees too much.

I don't answer. Instead, I pull open the drawer in the clock table. Inside, Julian's flashlight rolls around, and there's a small package of batteries in the back. I reach for the lamp, but nothing happens.

"No electricity," Angel says.

I take one of the batteries and slide it into the back of the clock, which begins to tick immediately.

Back in the living room, we sit in the dark. A spring from somewhere deep inside the couch suddenly pokes up between us, with an odd sound.

"Boing," Angel says, and we both laugh.

I like Angel's laugh; it's almost as if she's trying to catch her breath, sucks it in, and begins that small *uh-hu* again.

A streetlamp goes on—it's so strange to see it—shedding a path of light across the couch.

It isn't much, but enough to see a pile of mail scattered on the floor that's come in through a small slot in the door. I hesitate. Should I look at it?

It's not mine. And no one I know would write to Julian.

I glance at Angel. She has a sour look on her face. Her mouth is pursed like a bird's beak.

She reminds me of the old woman at home. I pull Felipe's pad toward me.

I Remember . . .

The house halfway down along the creek where the old woman lived. Her dark hair, shot with gray, was always pulled back in a bun, with pieces of hair flying into her face. She wore jeans that must have belonged to someone much bigger than she was.

She seemed to know when I was wading in the creek, bending over to run the cool water over my head, singing the frog song with my cracked-egg voice.

"I need peace," the woman yelled.

I looked up. She was standing at her door with a broom in her hand.

I backed away toward the bank of the creek. Was she going to swing at me with it?

Yes. She moved forward; I moved back. We were like the fighters in the ring I saw one summer night. If she landed with that broom, I'd be like the fighter who staggered around with a bump on his head the size of a rock.

But Julian splashed in behind me, scooped me up with both hands under my arms. We headed toward home along the creek, my feet hanging just above the water, laughing.

"Don't tell Mami," I said. "She'll want me to stay out of the creek."

"How about Abuelita?"

"Neither one."

We sat at the edge of the creek close to our house.

"That old woman is mean," I said.

"Abuelita says she's not mean; she's miserable."

"What do you say?" I asked.

Julian tilted his head. "She's a little wretched, I guess." *Wretched*. An English word. I could say it with my teeth together and my mouth barely moving. Wretched!

Julian skipped a stone into the water; then he ran his wet hands through his hair.

I didn't bother to tell him that his head was full of mud now.

Instead, lying there on the edge of the creek, we held our faces to the sun.

"Wretched," I said again.

chapter 8

food

Something is in my eyes—a pinprick of light; it's almost
blinding.

I raise my hand to push it away. And then I realize
it's morning. A sunbeam darts through the edge of the
curtain like an arrow, changing the color of the floor to
honey, the couch pillow to gold. The warmth on my face
reminds me of mornings at home.

It seems as if I slept for only moments. Angel
sprawled on the bed under Mami's quilt, and I threw
myself on the couch in the living room.

I look around. On the windowsill is a small pencil

drawing of a woman. It's Julian's work! The woman's face is turned away, but a thick braid rests on her shoulder.

Abuelita?

Propped up in the corner is the guitar.

I peek through a gap between the curtains. Outside someone is jogging down the street; then someone else, a bulky woman, marches by, holding a purse up to her chest. Two kids fight a duel with their backpacks, never stopping, probably on their way to school. A pickup truck lumbers down the street.

Everyone is awake.

Can they see me?

I tug the curtains together and the arrow of sunlight disappears.

I reach over and pull the guitar onto the couch with me, picking at each one of the six strings, hearing the difference in the sounds. One reminds me of the chimes at San Pablo Church at home. Another plinks high and thin: the meow of the stray cat as she greets me after school.

Angel stands in the kitchen doorway. "Be quiet, Diego. They'll hear you."

Diego! That was the name she whispered in the truck. "Who is that?"

Her hand goes to her mouth. "Nobody. You just looked like a guy who might be named Diego." She presses her lips together for a moment. Then she shakes her head. "My brother."

She rushes on. "If they hear you outside, they might think this place is haunted. They'll guess some idiot ghost is trying to make music."

I'm ready to ask her to tell me more. But I can see she doesn't want to talk about him. "I forgot," I say instead. "You never read what I had to say about Julian."

She goes into the kitchen and I follow her. I put the pad on the table and open it to the Julian section.

She doesn't reach for it. She doesn't even look interested.

If only I could look up and see Julian sitting at the table, or cooking at the stove. From the window, I see the backyard, the alley, and in the distance, just a hint of what might be a forest.

"I have to eat," Angel says. "We have to eat."

I glance at her. Her face is white as milk. And I feel it too now, a hollow pain in my stomach.

Yesterday we ate sandwiches that Felipe put together for us in the truck, but we've had nothing since.

"We can't go to a store yet," Angel says. "It's too early. People will wonder why we're not in school."

I miss school. That's a surprise.

She begins to go through the cabinets, running her fingers over the shelves, searching. She finds something and smiles back at me, holding up a can.

It's soup with a picture of a bowl, steam rising in a swirl above vegetables and rice and meat. My mouth waters.

Angel is way ahead of me. While I clean up the cereal and pick up the shards of the bowl that I broke last night, she rummages through the drawers, pulls out a can opener and a pair of spoons, and puts the can of soup on the burner.

But nothing happens. The stove doesn't work. I fiddle with the knobs, then shrug. "No electricity. Right!"

We stare at the can with its picture of chicken and carrots. I imagine the dark soup simmering, then bubbling around the edges, the wonderful salty smell of it filling the kitchen, the whole house.

"We'll eat it cold," Angel says.

She opens it and brings the can to the table, holding it as if it were a baby, careful not to spill even one drop.

She sets it down exactly in the center between the two of us. "I warn you—" Her freckles dot her nose; her cheeks are sunburned. "I'm a fast eater."

"Don't worry," I say, "I'll beat you."

She grins. We dip in our spoons, but we don't try to race each other. We're just glad we have enough to eat. We keep going until every piece of vegetable, every tiny grain of rice, every shred of meat is gone. Then I tip the can and hold it out. "Go ahead," I tell her. "Take the last sip."

And she does, a drop sliding down her chin. She rolls her thumb over it and puts it in her mouth. "I never tasted anything so good."

I nod, running my tongue over my lips. I stare out the kitchen window, at the tree branches that bend toward me.

But where's Julian? I have to start looking now. "Maybe you'll spell out a couple of words in English for me so I can start looking."

"Leave me alone for a while," she says. "I can't be doing stuff like that all the time."

What's the matter with her now? Maybe she's thinking about her brother. Maybe she's thinking about home.

Never mind. I go into the living room. I think of the building Julian was working on. I'll find it.

Haven't I found my way here, thousands of miles?

chapter 9

the ghost building

With the taste of soup still in my mouth, I say, "Angel, I have to go out for a while."

"People will wonder why you're not in school. I told you that before, Matty. We'll have to go to the store later."

She thinks she's my mother.

I press my lips between my teeth. And then I say it slowly, my words spaced, and I can hear the anger in my voice. "I have come here, all these miles, to find my brother, to make sure he's all right."

I brush away thoughts of prison or death. "I'm the

only one to help him, Angel. If I get caught, there's nothing I can do about it. Not one thing. It will just have to be. And no, I'm not going to the store right now."

"Where, then?" she says, checking the cabinet for food again.

"He was working on a building near here. I want to see it. Maybe I'll find something." I shrug. "I don't know."

"I'll come with you. I'm good at this kind of thing."

I take a breath, and then two or three more, calming myself. "You don't have to do that. You might get caught. People will think you should still be in school."

"What am I supposed to do all day? Stir a pot on the stove that doesn't work?" She grins, surprising me. "Look at a blank TV?"

"You can't sit still for a minute."

"So I'm coming." She flips her hair off her neck. "It's hot." And then, "Where is it?"

"I'm thinking." I turn away from her before she can say anything to that, and open the back door slowly to glance outside. No one is in the yard, which stretches across three houses. No one is in the alley beyond that. "Come on." For once I'm the one who's in charge.

We scurry across the yard and down the alley. I try to remember what Tomàs might have said about the building.

On a busy street?

No. It wasn't that.

Maybe stories. Yes. Ten stories high.

And the name of the avenue . . . No, he didn't say that either. He said it would be the tallest building in the town.

We stop at the end of the alley, hesitating, and look up. Not far away is a building with scaffolding. . . . We crane our necks. It looks ghostly with floors missing. Sunny blue sky filters in here and there.

We keep going past rows of shops; in dusty glass windows, we see piles of summer shirts, sneakers, and men's jackets on hangers.

Angel and I glance at each other as we pass the food store. We can smell something. . . .

Meat and salads, a whiff of garlic and onions, a vat with pickles swimming in vinegar at the door.

Angel can't resist. The door is open. She walks inside and stands there as I motion to her to come back outside.

The man behind the counter watches her, but at last she backs out the door. "That's my favorite place right now," she whispers as we circle around a man stuffing a huge sandwich in his mouth; it drips tomatoes and mayonnaise.

Next to me, Angel hurries. She's thinking about being caught. She's right again. People may look at me and think *Immigrant. Illegal immigrant. Wetback.*

I step out on the street and cross to the other side. Angel follows, hurrying away from the food store where the man in the apron stands at the window.

And then we're running.

Flying.

Now the tall building is only blocks away.

We reach that corner and stop to take a breath. In front of us is a gray slatted fence. The building isn't finished, not nearly.

But where are the workers?

I stretch my neck looking, and shiver thinking about being up so high, balancing myself on the beams.

Angel moves two of the fence slats aside and squeezes herself through to the work site.

"Not a good idea." I whisper, in case anyone is around. "Come back."

She pays no attention. She just keeps going.

All right. I'll do the same thing.

I duck my head and go through the fence. Inside, I search for friendly faces, for faces that look like mine, with dark eyes, dark hair, smiling faces. But I don't see anyone. And there's no noise: no sound of hammer and drills, of workers on platforms.

But there is someone. A watchman? He looks a little like me, but much older, with lines slashed across his forehead. He puts down a newspaper and stands, staring, then comes toward me.

I take a chance and speak in Spanish. "I'm looking for my brother Julian."

The man shakes his head.

"He worked here, before . . ."

"Before," the man repeats in Spanish. "There's no one working now. Everyone is gone, and the building might never be finished."

"But maybe you knew my brother," I begin, but something makes me turn. On the other side of the fence I see a police car, turret turning, red and blue lights flashing. Two policemen burst out of the car, shout, *"No trespassing!"* and come through the fence, slats breaking off.

chapter 10

the chase

Angel darts one way, and I go another.

I duck under a girder, just as the security man did, and then I'm climbing high.

My mouth is dry; my throat burns from the dust that rises from the building. My breath is loud and ragged; my hands reach for something that will help pull me up.

I try not to look down, because if I do, I'll paste myself to one of the girders and stay up here for the rest of my life.

But I can't help it. I have to look now that I'm on the seventh or eighth floor, or maybe even higher.

Below me, the world tilts; I close my eyes to stop the dizziness, and when I open them again, I see stores, rows of houses, maybe even the one that had been Julian's, and in the distance, a train station.

In the other direction, the policemen chase Angel as she darts down the street away from them.

On the street, a woman shades her eyes, looking up at me.

How will I ever get down? The wind is strong, pulling at me. How will I let go of this girder, with the world spinning below?

"One step at a time," a voice says.

My eyes are closed, but I'm sure it's the watchman who has followed me up here.

I may not be able to move, but I can talk. "My brother Julian was here." I shout a little against the wind.

"Illegal, like some of the others?" the man says.

I nod.

"I have a green card, so I can work here," he says.

I can't believe we're talking as if our feet were on the ground. The wind wants to sweep me away from the girder I'm straddling, my sweaty hands grasping it in front of me.

I duck my head, reminded of the top of the train I rode north, the wind pulling at my shirt, my jeans, my hair, burning my face.

The watchman isn't bothered. He steps along the girder and comes toward me, both hands free. "A while ago," he yells, "someone notified the police that there were many illegals here. A few were sent to prison." He shrugs. "And maybe deported later."

I manage to raise my head to take a quick look at him. "My brother?"

He shakes his head. "I'm sorry, I don't know."

There's no help here, and I don't even know how I'll ever get back down.

But he sees how afraid I am. "Just slide over. That's it, come toward me."

I can barely move.

"You're doing fine." I hear the smile in his voice. "You may even get a job working on high floors somewhere."

"Never." I try to smile too.

I edge along behind him until we come to some kind of elevator. It's nothing but a floor with a metal railing around the edges. You could fall right through.

"Just ease yourself on," he says.

I think I'll never be able to take the step that will put me on that elevator. But somehow I do.

And instead of standing at the edge of the platform, as the worker is doing, one hand relaxed on the railing, I crawl onto the floor and lie there, my hands close to his feet, ready to grab them if I feel as if I'm going to fall.

We begin to move. I don't open my eyes until we get to the ground floor. And when we do, I see that woman below, a large clip in her hair. The woman who's tall and thin, who glances up at me, and then away. I think she's crying, but probably not for me.

"A million thanks," I tell the watchman, standing at last. "My brother's name . . ."

"I know," he says. "Julian."

"My name is Mateo. If you ever see him, tell him I'm at his house."

"I will," he says. "I wish you luck. The absolute best of luck."

I raise my hand in a half wave as I walk away, but then he calls after me. "Hey, kid."

I turn. Has he remembered something?

I wait to hear what he has to say, heart pounding. *Don't let it be prison.*

"Some of the others . . . like us," he says, "work at a factory."

He points with his thumb. "It's this road, straight out of town. It's a terrible place; they make fertilizer. Only the most desperate try it, and most of them don't last. But it's possible that your brother is working there, or that someone knows him."

"Thank you," I tell him. "It's great that you remembered."

"Not so great if he's there."

Julian, who hates to be indoors, who wants to breathe the fresh air or the clean smell of the creek!

I thank the man again, and then I run back along

the avenue. I have to find Angel. In front of me is the food store with its delicious smells, and now the man with the apron is standing outside. I hesitate for the barest second because the apron reminds me so much of the one Abuelita wears with the loops tied around her neck.

The man sees me and smiles. "Hi." He raises a bottle of water to his mouth.

I try out my English. "Hello." Did I say it right?

The man grins. He drops the bottle and the water spills all over the sidewalk.

I dive for the bottle and hand it to him. "Good kid," he says.

"Yes," I say, and he grins again.

Then I lope toward the house. I wonder for the first time who owns it and whether he'll ever come to check on things.

I can't imagine what will happen to us if he does. I hurry now, hoping I'll find Angel there before me, safe. I think of her laugh, her bossiness, and get cold all through when I wonder if the police have caught her.

I move much more cautiously, making sure there are no police cars in front of me, no one following me.

chapter 11

waiting

How long have I been sitting here at the kitchen table, glancing out the window, waiting for Angel?

Suppose she's been caught! What will I do if she's in prison?

I won't let myself think that. Instead, I think about my stomach rumbling. I'm so hungry.

I stand up and peer into the cabinets, rubbing my hands over the shelves, but there's nothing there. Not even a crumb.

I hear the door creak open and turn.

It's Angel!

She must know from my face how glad I am. But she looks terrible. Her face is dusty, the back of her shirt is torn, and her hair is more knotted than ever.

She goes to the sink and turns on the faucet. She puts her head underneath and gulps down water. "I didn't want to come back here right away. I ran and ran, and after a while they stopped following me. There were trees, a small forest of evergreens, looking so cool, so I hid there. But I knew you'd be waiting."

She wipes her mouth with her fist. "I circled around the streets, watching, making sure no one was paying attention to me." She grins then. "I knew you'd be here, and I didn't want you to get in trouble either."

I grin back at her, and then we're quiet for a moment.

"Where's Diego?" I blurt out before I even realize what I'm saying.

"I don't know." Her eyes fill. Angel crying? She turns away.

I try something else. "Why are you here? Why are you helping me?"

"You were lying in the desert sand. I could see the back of your head, your hair poked out, just like his. No matter how he combed it. For just that second, I thought—"

"That I was your brother. Is he missing too?"

"Not missing." She stands by the window, looking out. "Enough." *All right*, I tell myself. *For now.*

"We have to have money for food," she says. "We'll go through this whole house. Even at home, there's always money when you least expect it, under the bed, on the floor of the closet."

I think of the money from Abuelita. I promised myself I wouldn't use it, not unless I was desperate. I reach inside my pocket, feeling the two bills. Maybe now is the time. But will I be able to use Mexican money here?

Angel runs her fingers through her hair. "You'll see. We'll find something. Then we'll clean ourselves up and wait until school has to be over for the day. We'll just be two kids shopping."

It sounds all right, but I can't imagine that there's money here.

"Which room do you want to search?"

"The bedroom, I guess."

I wander inside and touch Mami's quilt. Then I crawl under the bed, the dust balls rolling around me, making me sneeze, and only find an old newspaper and a sock.

I try the closet, crawling on the floor in there, too. Nothing.

Back in the kitchen, I raise my shoulders. "No good."

She marches into the bedroom. "It takes longer than that to search. Did you look under the pillows, the sheets, the mattress?"

I shake my head.

"The closet shelves? The jeans pockets? Especially

the pockets." She taps the door molding hard, and goes back into the kitchen. "Get with it, Matty."

The pockets. Of course. I turn them inside out, but they're empty. Standing on tiptoes, I run my hands over the dusty shelves. Next I pull the bed apart. Nothing.

I sink down under the window, leaning back against the wall and the dusty curtains.

I hear a crackle. I reach back. Something's in the hem of the curtain. I work it out and sit back.

It's a very small, tight roll of American money!

I rub the bills. How much is it? Not much, I can tell. It must be Julian's money; Mami used to hide money in her bedroom curtains too. He won't mind; I'll tell him as soon as I find him anyway.

I stand up and go into the kitchen. Angel has the oven door open. Her head's inside as she searches.

She reminds me of the girl in that fairy tale about two children and a witch.

"I'm with it, Angel," I tell her.

She backs out and kneels on the floor, her hands out to show me how filthy they are.

I hold out the money.

"Yes!" Then she glances at the window. "It's late, dark. We can't go to the store until tomorrow."

I frown. "That man will remember you."

"What man?"

"The owner of the food store. You had to walk inside

and stand there. Maybe he thought you were going to steal something," I say. "I'll go alone." Maybe the man will remember me too. But he was friendly.

She sinks down at the table. "I guess you're right." But it's almost as if the words are forced out of her.

And then she teaches me a few words. *"Beans,"* she says, and I repeat it.

She slaps the table. "Not beens. *Beeeeenzzzz.*"

"That's what I said."

"Apples."

I say that too but she's not satisfied. "Just wait until tomorrow. He must be closed now. But then we'll pick things up."

"Maybe you should write it all down in English."

"Waste of time," she says. "You're driving me crazy."

Good.

chapter 12

the store

It's morning. We can't wait to eat any longer.

"Kids will be going to school," I say.

"If the store owner asks, say *holiday*."

"Holy day?"

She slaps her head. "Say *'I've been sick.'*"

"Sick. I've got it."

I go into the bathroom and turn on the water in the shower. It's icy cold, but there's soap, and I try to clean my clothes. I have to look decent.

I dry myself, and the clothes. Better, much better. I see the old Mateo in the mirror.

I walk along the street; kids weave back and forth.

One tosses a ball to his friend, and I duck to get out of the way. No one pays attention to me, not even the police in a car that rolls slowly down the street.

If only I could go to that factory right now. But we both have to eat. I can't imagine Julian in a place like that. I picture his face, the time he planted a small tree out back, and painted that same tree on our bedroom wall. I hear him singing that frog song. What else about him? I hear him say: *"A house in the woods. Watching the fox at night, the geese and birds in the morning."*

Coming along next to me, someone says, "That kid is talking to himself."

He means me.

I have just time to see his face and sandy hair. He rams into me, his elbow sharp against my ribs, and I feel that old pain from the desert. My feet go out from under me and I sprawl on the ground. He steps around me and dashes away, and I see . . .

Do I really see?

With both hands, he holds bills over his head.

My money!

He's already at the corner. He turns and is gone.

I lie there for another moment, catching my breath. It's too late to go after him, even though he isn't bigger than I am. If I see him again, I'll push him against a wall. I'll go through his pockets. I'll take my money back.

Ridiculous. He'll probably spend the money within the next few minutes.

I scramble to my feet, holding my side. I'm so hungry, and what about Angel? I think of beans and bananas, cold soup. Abuelita's chicken.

I think about stealing. The food store is just down the street and outside is a bin with fruit and vegetables. I'm fast; I could scoop up two pears, or a bunch of carrots, before the man in the apron could come after me.

I see the man's kind face.

I can't steal.

Something crosses my mind, a vague memory. Something about Julian. Yes, I'll write about it when I can.

I walk back to the house slowly and go in the back door. Angel is still sitting at the table. She looks up and it's almost impossible to tell her what's happened. "I'm going to try for a job."

"Where's the food, Matty?"

"Someone took my money."

Her eyes widen. Then she really looks at me. She must see how sorry I am, how terrible I feel. "We'll think of something."

And then the memory crosses my mind again, the quickest thought. I raise my hand to my forehead, but it's gone.

Something about . . . a secret.

That makes me think of Angel. What is it she doesn't want to tell me? But before I can try to ask again, she says, "Are you writing something about me in that notebook?"

"Sure. Why not?"

She doesn't answer. Head high, she walks away.

I stand at the back door. What should I do next? I go into the living room, and my notebook is gone. I know how to look for things now. I look all over the place.

It's in the kitchen litter basket.

"Why would you do that?" I yell. "Why?"

"It's a nuisance. In my way."

"It belongs to me." I'm still shouting.

"Sorry." She raises one shoulder. "You're making so much noise. Do you want the police to come?"

I take a breath. It's all too much. I take the notebook and toss it on the table.

"Sorry," she says again. "I guess I shouldn't have done that."

"No. But now I need to get a job, to get some money so we can eat."

She nods, sits at the table. "I'd go, but the police saw my face. Maybe I'd better stay in here."

She's right. I tell her I have to learn English. "Teach me some words, Angel."

"What words?"

I say them slowly in my own language. "I need a job, please. I'm a good worker."

She looks up at the ceiling. Is she trying not to laugh at me?

"We'll starve to death if I don't work." I push away thoughts of Mami and Abuelita cooking in our kitchen. What are they eating? Will the tablecloths bring them enough food for a while? Are they as hungry as we are? And poor Lucas.

Angel says the words over and over. They seem strange on my tongue; they don't fit in my mouth.

Angel raises her hand to her mouth to hide her smile as I repeat them.

Fifty times?

Sixty?

Then I hear myself getting closer to what she's saying until, at last, I have it.

"*Ineedajob.*" I take a breath. Count one-two-three-four. "*I'magoodworker.*"

"Slow down." Angel nods, looking pleased with the way I sound. We go through other words: *string beans* and *meat, sweep* and *dust.*

By this time it's afternoon, after school. And I'm ready. I don't have to think about *holy days* or *I've been sick.*

"You'll get a job," Angel says. "Don't worry."

"At that grocery store." I feel as if I just might be able to do it.

I straighten my collar and smooth down my every-which-way hair, even though it pops up again almost immediately. "How do I look?"

"Good." She leans forward. "Matty, hurry. I don't think I've ever been so hungry." She shakes her head and speaks in English. "You look spiffy."

Spiffy.

I keep saying that to myself as I go to the kitchen door. It has a great sound.

I hop off the back step and head down the street counting as I go, four blocks one way, and then turn at the wide avenue with zebra stripes.

And there's the store on the corner. Up on top there's a sign: *Deli*. It blinks back and forth in orange.

I give my hair one last pat, take a breath, and open the door.

I walk in, looking at the rows of cans with pictures of oranges and pineapples. I pass a bin that has a few sad-looking plantains, pale, as if they didn't have a chance to ripen in a warm sun. Behind the glass counter are lumps of meat: red and pink. There are chickens too, pathetic things with skinny tan legs.

The man with the Abuelita apron watches me from behind the counter. His face is friendly, and he smiles under his droopy black mustache. He nods as I walk toward him, my hands behind my back, my fingers crossed. He remembers me.

I say the words slowly, to be sure he understands them. I even try an extra bit. "I swip," I say, and make sweeping motions to be sure I have it right.

Maybe not. The man's mustache is quivering. He's ready to laugh. "Sweeeep." He draws out the middle part, just the way Angel did.

"Dust." I wave my hand at the fruit stuck in cans. And then I'm finished. This language wears me out.

The man bites his mustache. "What's your name?" he asks slowly.

Ah, I know that. I give him my northern name. "Matty."

He points to himself. "Sal." He nods toward the broom in the back hallway.

"Yes?"

He says something back. Who know what it is? But I take a chance and dive for the broom, glancing back at him to see if he's nodding, or frowning. But someone has come into the store. He turns away and I begin to sweep.

In the factory, Miguel used to scream at Damian and me. "That's the way you sweep? Everything just piled up in the corner?"

Damian would wait until Miguel went to bother someone else. Then he'd push all the dirt into another corner. We'd laugh, thinking Miguel would never know the difference. And sometimes he didn't. I remember once I fell over the broom, and even he had to grin.

But in this deli with its blinking sign, with dust all over the soup cans, I sweep enormously, back and forth, until there's not a speck on the floor, and Sal with the Abuelita apron is smiling. "Good job," he says.

He's mixing up my words, but that's all right.

Without asking, I find a dust cloth in back. I dust every one of those cans of soup, and string beans, and corn.

And then, a surprise.

Sal beckons me into the back. "Supper." He waves his hand at the table.

There's food on a paper plate: a roll with ham and cheese hanging out the edges. There's a long skinny pickle and a can of soda. I haven't had so much to eat since I left home. My mouth waters.

I'm not sure it's for me.

"Go ahead," he says.

I don't sit at the table. Instead, I lean forward, standing, and ram half the sandwich into my mouth. I look at the rest, thinking of Angel. "Home?" I ask, pointing.

Sal shakes his head. "Eat it all," I think he says. He goes out to the front and a few minutes later he's back with another sandwich, three bottles of soda, three of water, and the same friendly soup in a can that Angel and I love. "Home," Sal says with a sweep of his arm.

I gulp down the soda, then keep my hands in my pocket so I don't devour the other sandwich.

He even gives me some money.

Wait until Angel sees all this.

I duck my head; I wish I knew what to say. "Spiffy," I tell him at last, knowing he's giving me much more than I deserve for a little sweeping and dusting.

He nods, and I wonder if he knows I'm illegal.

And then I'm on the way home, carrying the bag of food. I'm going to sit on the couch with a soda, as if I'm rich. What will I write? I think about the boy who took my money today, and a time long ago, when I took something too. I'll write about that memory. Why not?

I Remember . . .

I stole once. It was after we'd eaten, my homework finished, and I splashed through the creek, dragging my feet along the sand.

And there was that miserable old woman's house, her broom resting on the porch, both the woman and the broom ready to come after me.

This time I'd go after the broom.

I crept up on the porch, my bare feet leaving wet prints, and I reached, reached farther for it.

Then it was in my hand. I backed down the step and ran along the edge of the creek in the growing darkness.

"Too bad, old woman," I whispered to myself, and threw the broom into the high weeds that lined the creek.

It was so easy . . .

Until I told Julian.

"We can't do that, Mateo," he said. "What does she have but her house, her broom? No family. No one to care about her."

We went back to look for the broom, but it wasn't there.

"Maybe she found it," I said.

"I don't think so." He ran his hands through his hair. "It's here somewhere, but it's too dark."

Julian took the money he'd been saving in his sock and bought her a broom, a much better one that wasn't filthy and falling apart. He carried it up to her porch with me in back of him.

The old woman stuck out her lip, not a bit grateful. But later Julian said, "Why should she be grateful? We're the ones who caused her broom to be lying in the weeds somewhere."

That was Julian. "We're the ones," he'd said, when he knew it wasn't any of his fault.

I took the coin Abuelita had given me for my name day and slipped it into his sock that night.

chapter 13

the factory

The bedroom door is closed the next morning, so Angel must be sleeping. I tear a piece of paper from the notebook and scribble a message:

> *A—*
> *Went to look at a factory. Don't worry.*
> *I won't get caught.*

I leave it in the living room on the scarred table in front of the couch.

It's a straight road, but it stretches a long way in front of me. It's empty, no people, no cars, and after a while it loses its city look: no longer cement, but a dirt road that sends up swirls of dust and grit that I feel on my tongue as I walk along. I'm slower now. The sun feels as if it's burning a hole through the top of my head.

But then, ahead, I see evergreen trees, odd shaped and thin, packed together. They send cool shade across the road, and a wonderful piney smell.

On the way back, I'll step into that forest. But for now, I hope that I'm on my way to Julian.

A few minutes after I pass the forest, the smell changes. It's a choking kind of smell that makes me want to cough, that makes me want to breathe through my mouth so I don't have to take in that thick odor of fertilizer.

The factory. I see a long, low gray building with a chimney spewing yellow smoke. I watch for someone to come outside, someone who looks friendly enough to ask.

I wait a long time until I hear a whistle. It's so loud that I put my hands over my ears. The doors open; men and women pour out, coughing, and head for benches with their lunches.

Could I just go over there? I look around. No policemen anywhere that I can see. I make myself walk to one of the benches. The four women sitting there glance up, sandwiches in their hands.

I clear my throat, tasting the fertilizer. "I'm looking for my brother," I say in Spanish, my voice hoarse.

One of the women speaks, her voice as hoarse as mine. "What's his name?" And another, "What does he look like?"

And the one sitting at the end of the bench, her hair straight down her back, says, "He looks like this kid, I bet. What's your name?"

I can hardly breathe. "Mateo."

"Dark eyes . . ." She raises her hand to her head. "Hair . . ."

She doesn't want to say every-which-way hair.

"And," she goes on, "his name is Julian."

I sink down on the edge of the bench next to her. I can't talk. I can't open my mouth. I can't say a word.

She takes a bite from her sandwich. "You remember?" she asks the others.

They shake their heads, chewing now, but they look at me carefully.

The woman knows. I watch her. I wait.

"He worked here, I remember," she says. "A nice boy. A good boy. Gone now." She takes another bite.

My words rush out. "But where is he?"

"I don't know, child."

"Which way did he go?"

I can see she's becoming irritated, but I can't help that.

I point toward the road. Is it the way I've come, or do I have to go farther?

She tosses the paper bag over her shoulder. It hits the litter basket, falls back, and lands on the ground. If it hadn't been for Sal's food, I would have gone after it, eaten that crust and been glad to have it.

But one of the other women takes pity on me. "I think this way." She points to the road, to the way I've come.

"Do you remember anything else?" Any tiny piece of information, almost like one of the chunks of chicken in Mami's soup, will make a difference.

But the factory whistle blasts again. The women stand. They have to go back to work.

Next to me, a woman puts her hand on my shoulder. "I think he said he owes someone."

chapter 14

the pine forest

I hear the slap of my sneakers—*He owed someone.* And why do I keep thinking of the miserable woman with the broom?

The sound of my breath—*What kind of trouble is he in?*

Ahead are the green trees, bending toward me on both sides of the road.

I run off the road, onto a much softer bed of sand and needles; I breathe in the sharp smell of the pines and slow down.

Julian would love this spot. At home, Mami will be

sewing at the kitchen table, worrying about him, worrying about money . . .

Worrying about me.

I touch Abuelita's medal.

The wind whispers to the branches with a sound like breaking glass. I veer toward a small path, putting one foot in front of the other.

Something moves.

I stand entirely still.

It's a deer, her color almost orange under the trees, her tail white, her ears high. She reaches up to pull a branch closer to her so she can nibble at the leaves.

For just that moment, all the worry melts out of me. How lucky I am to see her, to be here in this hidden world, to write about it someday.

I hear something and move behind the nearest tree, a tall one with zigzag branches. A twig gently scratches my cheek, and I reach up to touch it.

There's silence.

I wait for what seems forever; then I raise my head slowly, my hands grasping the trunk.

The deer is still there, no longer feeding. Her head is up, her ears twitching, her great dark eyes staring. She's heard what I heard.

There's a screech. I jump, almost darting away, then stare up into the tree. A large bird perches near the top, its yellow talons wrapped around a branch; its eyes are hooded, angry-looking. A hawk, I think. It blinks slowly; then it glides away and the deer jumps effortlessly over a fallen branch.

Both are gone and I'm alone.

But not quite.

I hear footsteps now, scratchy against the pine needles, so I stay where I am. A woman comes down the narrow path. Her streaked hair is swept up in back with a comb, and she's wearing boots.

She moves forward away from me, dropping fistfuls of seeds as she walks. The seeds are black, striped; I know what they are: tall yellow sunflowers grow from those seeds.

I follow the woman.

Why do I do things like this? It will surely get me caught.

Still, I raise one foot and then the other as I walk, so the swish of the sand and the pine needles is quiet.

The woman takes a long time going down that winding path, the pine bending over us. She stops, the seeds spilling through her fingers.

Something hisses.

I stand on tiptoes to see a gray striped cat, its back arched. It's much larger than the stray at home. It must be a bobcat.

The woman waits as the bobcat disappears up a narrow path, thick with fallen needles, and she follows slowly, giving it room.

I go after her, watching as she tosses more seeds; then I take another path, narrower still, veering away from her to be sure she doesn't turn and spot me.

I circle around a few straggly bushes, arms out to feel the branches, and then jump over a silvery rock.

I picture Julian here. I remember once walking along the creek together. I took big steps, trying to keep up with him, and he pointed to a silver fish swimming along, its tail flipping out of the water.

Julian and I smiled at each other, picturing it safe from our fishing poles. *Be safe, Julian.*

Just beyond me is a pile of gray rocks, and a narrow opening.

A cave?

I walk toward it quietly, shuffling through millions of old pine needles and sand, staring at the narrow slit in the rocks.

Suppose an animal lives in that cave?

The bobcat? A coyote?

I have to go back. Maybe I could work at the food store again, although it doesn't need sweeping now; it doesn't need dusting.

And Angel will be waiting for me. I wonder about her.

All I know after all this time is that she has a brother, Diego, and yes, a grandfather.

It's hard to find my way out. One path leads to another, and then to another.

I begin to run again, the pine needles scuffing up. But I'm not so far from the road, I'm sure of it; I hear the sound of cars rolling along on the pavement, the beeping of a horn, a dog barking faintly.

I follow those sounds until I find the road, a car whizzing past.

I head for home.

Home?

It's amazing that I'm thinking about the house that way. We shouldn't even be there. And suppose we're caught?

What a long day—the factory, the women having sandwiches at the picnic table, one of them knowing Julian. I think of the pines as I head away from them, losing that clean, clear smell. I wish I could show the forest to Julian.

But then I stop. Julian lived here, right in that house, going back and forth to the factory.

He'd have seen this pine forest.

Wouldn't he have walked here the way I have?

And if he's still somewhere nearby, wouldn't he come back to walk along those needle-strewn paths?

Unless he's gone.

But there's something else: the woman with her streaked hair caught up in a large clip, her boots, the sunflower seeds she dropped for the animals in the forest.

I've seen her before, haven't I?

I stop in the middle of the road, the black tar sticky in the heat. She was at the unfinished building, standing there.

And she was crying.

I wonder why.

chapter 15

angel

As I turn into the alley, I see a man and a woman standing halfway down, looking up . . .

Toward our house?

The woman has a camera. Is she taking a picture? Do they want to move in?

My heart bounces up into my throat.

I back away and go around to the front. Opening the door quietly, I slip inside.

Halfway through the living room, I hear the bedroom door slam. It's so loud, I wonder if the man and woman outside can hear it. Do they wonder who's slamming a door in an empty house?

"Angel?" I whisper.

She doesn't answer.

I put my nose up to the closed door. "People are outside."

She opens the door a crack, her eyes flashing.

"In the alley," I say. "Two of them."

"I don't care."

I push my foot in so she can't slam the door again. "What's the matter with you?"

"You're the matter," she says. "You've been gone forever. How was I to know if you weren't caught somewhere? Never coming back?" She shoves her hair behind her ears.

I look toward the living room and see my note on the table. An empty soda bottle rests on top of it. How could she not have seen it?

"Look." I point to the note. "I told you where I was going."

She shakes her head.

"Under the soda bottle."

She pushes the door open, cranes her neck, and glances at the table. "I didn't see it."

She had to have seen it.

I hesitate.

I look from the table and then at her.

She steps away from the door, then tries to close it.

"No." I'm almost shouting, my foot holding the door open. "Tell me what's going on with you."

"Nothing at all." Her nose is in the air. She sees that I'm not going to let her close the door, so she pulls it open and stamps into the kitchen as if I don't exist.

I lean my head against the wall for a moment, trying to figure out what to do. Then I grab my writing book and follow her. I slide onto a chair, the book in front of me. I act as if everything is all right. "I'm going to write some words here." I smooth out a page. "It's time I learned more English."

"A waste of time."

"You don't have to write anything, Angel. Just spell out a few words." I slide the book toward her.

"I'm too tired."

"You could help me," I begin, but I'm saying it to her back.

She's gotten up from her chair and lifted the curtain at the bottom of the window an inch or so. She stares out at the alley. "There's no one there."

"They're gone, then." I'd forgotten all about them. "Help me, Angel." I try to say it so she doesn't know how angry I am.

She sinks down on the chair again. "You should learn

to say the words before you write them down, Matty."
Fresh voice.

I'm ready to explode. "All you do is hang out."

She uncurls her bare feet from underneath her and goes into the living room.

"You could just—" I begin, but she brushes past me and goes back into the bedroom. She doesn't bother to shut the door and I can see she's grabbing her bag and the sweater she picked up in the desert.

Stamping into the kitchen, she takes a little of Sal's money from the table. "I'll pay you back; don't worry." She slams out the door.

I watch from the window. She runs along the alley, her bag bouncing on her shoulder, and turns the corner. Where is she going?

I can do that too.

I go out the front door.

It's really late now, and the streets are empty: no people, no cars. It's not that dark, though, so I run all the way back to the pine trees.

I take that small path, breathing in the sharp piney smell to calm myself. A small animal crashes away from me.

I sink down and huddle under one of the trees. What's wrong with Angel?

Last night, everything was different. She pulled me

outside in the yard, past the junk that littered the lawn, and showed me small cactus flowers that were blooming under a rusted-out table.

"You can hardly see them in the dark," I said.

She nodded. "I couldn't wait until tomorrow, though. Don't they look beautiful?"

She was smiling at me, happy.

Weird.

And another thing. She cleaned the whole kitchen during the morning while I was gone; I saw that. She scrubbed the last of the cereal stains off the floor and the fingerprints off the cabinets.

I sit under the tree for a long time. I'm so quiet now that I hear the small noises the forest makes: the swish of the branches, a soft hoot. I look up slowly, moving my head an inch at a time, and I see an owl, feathers so soft, yellow eyes blinking.

Suppose Angel doesn't come back?

Angel, who helped me cross the river, who shared soup with me.

Angel with her bag over her shoulder.

Was she heading toward the train station?

I picture her climbing onto a train just before it begins to move.

Angel sitting on one of those seats next to the window, napping while the engine carries her south.

Angel gone.

Would she do that?

I scramble up and run through the trees, down the narrow path where I saw the deer. I veer onto the street, my sneakers slapping the pavement, my breath loud in my ears.

I see that woman again; this time her hair hangs straight down her back. She carries an umbrella, swinging it along in the dark.

Never mind that she sees me, an illegal. I'm fast and I'm away from her.

Angel!

I have to make sure Angel is still there.

chapter 16

the train station

I circle a telephone pole and a pair of garbage cans, dash across the yard, and push open the kitchen door, not even bothering to close it behind me. Fingers crossed, I call, "I'm back, Angel," and stop to catch my breath.

I walk through the house, holding my side. The bedroom is neat without Angel's bag and her things on the floor.

Empty.

Everything is completely quiet.

"Angel?" It almost sounds as if my voice is echoing. "It's Matty. I'm here."

Where is she?

In the kitchen, I sink onto a chair. She's going to take the train south. Maybe she'll go back over the border. She knows how to do that.

I race back through the living room, slip on the rug, right myself, and tear out the front door.

I don't care who sees me. . . .

I have to find her before she gets on a train.

I stumble over the curb, stubbing my toe. My eyes tear. I don't even know her last name.

Suppose I never see her again?

The train station is a block ahead now; I raise my head, searching. I take the steps to the platform two at a time, and slide onto the nearest bench, my chest heaving. Sit, I tell myself, just for a second.

From there, I can see the length of the station. It's totally empty; a few overhead lights cast a yellow glow across the platform and shine on the tracks. It's late; no one's there . . .

Except for the figure huddled on a wooden bench, under one of the lights, all the way down at the end.

I stare at the tracks. They run a long way, partners, next to each other, before they disappear into the dark. There's no train in sight. I have a few minutes to figure things out, so I stay where I am, thinking. What can I say that will make her come back?

But then I go toward her, still not sure what will

make her change her mind. I sit down next to her, but I can't think of a single word.

Her feet are up on the bench, her arms circling her knees. Her fingers and hair are so much cleaner than the first time I saw her.

"Let's go home," I say.

She doesn't answer.

"Come on, Angel."

She turns her head away.

"I don't even think there'll be a train this late."

She rests her head on her knees. "One will come along sooner or later, and I'll be on it." She shrugs. "I'll send the money back; you know I will."

She's been crying, and now tears slip down her cheeks. "Don't cry."

She brushes furiously at her cheeks. "I never cry."

"I'm sorry." I raise my shoulders, trying to think of what I've done.

"I don't belong here," she says.

I shake my head. "I don't either."

"I don't belong anywhere."

Belong. I can almost see Abuelita's thick gray braid swinging, her hands rough as she slips the medal and chain around my neck. Mami sings at the stove, turning to pop a spoonful of rice pudding into my mouth. There's Lucas spinning around, grinning at me. And outside, the cat purrs as she feels the sun on her back.

"Maybe you don't have to belong in a place," I say slowly. "Maybe it has to do with belonging to people."

"I don't have people," Angel says.

"Why aren't you home with . . ." I hesitate. "Your grandfather?"

She turns to me, her eyes huge, swimming with tears, her voice so low I can hardly hear her. "My brother, Diego, is my family, but now he's in the army." She wipes her eyes. "He says that will help him become a citizen; we'll live legally in Texas someday. We'll even bring our grandfather."

She stops talking, and I wait.

"Diego doesn't know that I'm not with our grandfather."

She looks at the tracks. Is that a train in the distance? "I can't even write to Diego. Can't write . . ." Her voice trails off. "I wanted to go to school so much."

The train wails. I grab her arm. No way is she going to get on that train.

But it seems as if she hasn't even heard the rumble on the tracks. "Just before my mother died, we were living in Texas, then Mexico, back and forth. I never knew my father. I was late starting school, but my teacher was friendly, even though she knew how far behind I was."

I reached for her hand.

"But then Diego and I were picking crops, so I didn't go to school. He took me to our grandfather's in Mexico, and I started school all over again. I was so tall, so much older than the others. The little kids in my class laughed at me. I just about knew the alphabet. I lasted only a few days."

She glances along the tracks, sees the train, and stands. I stand with her, still holding her hand.

She begins again. "My grandfather was furious with me. 'No one lives here who doesn't go to school.' I never told him I couldn't read. And after Diego left, we had our last argument. I walked out."

She raises her shoulders. "So I've been walking ever since, grabbing food here and there. Sometimes people help."

I shake my head.

"You see?" she says. "You see? I can't read. I can't write. And the odd part is that I love my grandfather. He feeds the animals outside, and when he holds out his hand, birds swoop down and rest on his wrist, eating small pieces of fruit."

I don't know what to say.

"I can't do anything," she whispers.

"You know all about the desert," I say. "And you swim better than anyone." I reach back and loop her bag over my arm. Still she doesn't move. "I'm here because of you, Angel."

The train explodes into the station with a blast of wind behind it. Bits of paper swirl onto the platform.

Whatever Angel says next is lost. We close our eyes against the dust that rises up from the tracks below.

"I'm really tired," I tell her.

"Mateo-Matty." She reaches into her pocket and pulls out Sal's money, the paper bill and silver coins clenched in her hands, and gives them to me.

I take them, because without them, she can't change her mind and take the train away from here.

We walk home together. Only a few cars are on the road, their lights beaming. The houses are dark; people are wrapped up in bed, sleeping.

At the back of the house, Angel stops. "You left the kitchen door open." She's almost back to her old self.

Inside, I close the door slowly, quietly. We stand there looking at each other. I reach into the closet and pull out a can of soup; I can almost taste tomatoes and onions.

"I have no more secrets," Angel says. "Not one."

I nod, opening the soup. Later I'll write a memory about Abuelita. I know now why Angel's so mean sometimes. I think about her grandfather and wonder if he wishes things were different.

I Remember . . .

Abuelita and I walked back along the creek road, carrying packages of fabric from the post office. They weren't so heavy, but they were bulky, and the sun beat down on us. I could hear her heavy breathing; she began to walk slower.

Halfway home, she tapped my shoulder. "Let's do this. . . ."

"What?"

Without answering, she put her package under a tree. In two seconds, her shoes came off, and her bare feet rested in the mud.

She grinned, and for the first time I could picture her as a young girl.

She went ahead of me, down to the creek, and splashed into the water, holding up the hem of her housedress. "Why are you waiting, my boy?"

I dropped my package on top of hers, slipped out of my sneakers and into the water right behind her, both of us saying "Ah" at the same moment.

As she reached down to splash me with a little water, we saw the miserable old woman walking along on the other side of the creek. She glanced at us and sniffed, then looked away as she kept going.

"Old witch," I whispered, thinking Abuelita would laugh. "Wretched."

"Poor thing," she said instead.

"Ha!" I cupped my hands and brought water up to trickle over my face.

"People who act tough, who act mean, are usually unhappy," she said, twisting the braid that hung over her shoulder. "And that one is surely unhappy. She has no one there to love." Abuelita turned her head. "And I have you. So lucky."

I was the lucky one. I knew that.

She looked serious. "I know you will be a writer; it's easy to see that. But remember you have to study people like that one." She pointed toward the road where the woman had disappeared. "And maybe," she said, "you'll understand."

After a while, we splashed our way out of the creek,

shaking ourselves off to dry. I grinned seeing her wet dress, her braid dripping.

"Yes, I was young once," she said.

"A thousand years ago," I teased.

She patted my cheek. "True," she said as I smiled up at her.

chapter 17

a chicken?

In the morning, before Angel wakes up, I tear a piece of paper out of the notebook. I'm not such a hot artist, but still I draw, erasing every two minutes: the head, the body, the stick-like legs. "Not bad," I tell myself, and write *la ciguena* underneath.

I tiptoe into the kitchen and prop it up on the table. Then I wait.

Angel comes in, rubbing her eyes and yawning; she stops. "What's that? A chicken?"

"Are you crazy? Does a chicken have legs two feet long?"

She's laughing now. "A stork. The worst-looking stork I've ever seen."

She touches the word. "What's this about?"

"Simple. You can read that: *la ciguena*. Take a good look and remember."

She cuts an apple Sal sent home and munches on slices as she looks at the stork, its chicken body, its pencil-thin legs. "So, one word," she says at last.

I go into the living room and pick up the mail on the floor: shiny papers with pictures of cars, all colors, all sizes, in a language I can't understand.

There's a small folder with red sweaters, and sweatshirts, and a picture of a woman wearing huge bracelets halfway up her arm. She reminds me of the woman I saw outside the unfinished building, the same woman who feeds the animals in the pine forest.

"Come and see something," I call into the kitchen.

She comes to the doorway and taps the molding. "What, Matty-Mateo?"

"I was thinking. Maybe today you'll learn some words. And I'll learn to speak English."

I hold my breath, afraid she'll be angry, but she just tilts her head and looks away. So I gather up the papers and spread them out on the floor. She hesitates, then sits across from me.

On top of a shiny car page, I spell out *car* in Spanish. "Simple," I say.

Angel bends over the page, writes *car* in shaky letters underneath.

From there we go to *eyeglasses*, to *sweater*, to *sweatshirt*, and she says them aloud in English as she writes.

"Car," I say. "Eyeglasses. Sweater."

But I want more, need more. She tells me outside words like *pine* and *sky* and *tree*. She tells me Sal words like *work, soup, please,* and a long piece that means *See you tomorrow, Sal.*

Now it's late afternoon and we have nothing left to eat, so I have to go to Sal's; I want to anyway. I splash water onto my face, and then I picture all of us squeezed in at the table at home, eating Mami's beans and rice, while Lucas plays the guitar, mouth full of food.

My stomach hurts with thinking.

I washed my T-shirt this morning, and it's still damp. But the sun is beating in the window, leaving patches of heat on the couch and the table, so I pull it on and the dampness feels terrific.

I leave Angel to write *car* and *eyeglasses* a million times.

It's even hotter outside. I walk along the streets with no one paying attention. I look for the kid who took my money, but he's nowhere around.

Sal's store is dim and cool from the air-conditioning. He's at the counter, putting containers of milk into a bag for someone.

When she turns, I see it's the woman who scattered sunflower seeds. She smiles at me and Sal raises his hand in a wave. "He's a good kid, that Matty," he tells her.

He grins at me and points to the back room. "Eat."

I know that word. I can taste the soft dough, the sugar thick on the outside, and the jelly hidden in the center. He's probably left juice there, too.

I go back for the broom, and stop to see what he's left for me. On a plate is a sugary cake. I take a bite of the soft dough; jelly is hidden in the center. I gulp down some of the juice, and then I sweep the back room. I take huge strokes, bending under the table to get up every crumb. Miguel at the factory wouldn't believe it.

My shirt is drying now, sticking to my ribs, when Sal comes back nodding. "Good job."

"Yes," I say, not sure what he means, but he has such a kind face. He must know that I'm illegal, and a word Angel said this morning: *undocumented* something. But he doesn't seem to mind.

"When," I begin. No. I shake my head. "What." Wrong again.

"Who," I say at last, pointing to the door.

"The woman?" he asks.

"Yes."

I dredge up the words. "She was . . ." The word *crying* comes to me. I begin again. "She was crying at the unfinished building."

"Elena," he says. "She owns the building."

"Owns?"

"It's hers. The police took away some of the workers that she'd already paid. She can't afford to hire others."

In my mind, I put it together. This is the person Julian worked for. She paid him, and Tomàs, and the others. The woman with a clip in her hair, and the black eyeglasses, crying over her building.

I begin to tell Sal about Julian slowly. I tell him in Spanish, putting in some English words that I somehow know.

He sinks back against the glass doors of the refrigerator that holds all the sad-looking chickens.

Sal raises his hand. He's trying to understand. "Your brother?"

"My brother. Missing."

I can't believe I know that word, *missing*, but I do, and I know he understands by the look on his face, the droop of his mustache. He tells me, "Sorry." He puts his large hand on my shoulder for a moment.

I swallow and begin to sweep again. And the long swishing sounds of the broom seem to say, *You'll find him. Don't worry. You'll find him somehow.*

If only that were true.

I finish everything and pick up the bag Sal has given me. "See you tomorrow," he says, and I nod.

I walk back to the house. It's late. Angel will be asleep, so I'll write again, write about Julian.

I Remember . . .

I'd stolen the broom, walked right up there on the stone path the old woman had made. Without meaning to, I scuffed up the stones, ruined her path. I was sorry about that.

The next day, Julian came home, his fishing pole over his shoulder, a mess of fish on a string for Mami to cook up for dinner.

"Not only the broom," he whispered so I was the only one to hear. "But you scattered her path."

I could hear the anger in his voice. "You did that, Mateo."

I didn't know what to say, and Julian shook his head and looked away from me.

We ate the fish that Abuelita fried, and carrots or pole beans, I guess, I don't remember. But instead of enjoying the usual sweet taste of the poor fish who'd been swimming in the creek just an hour ago, I could hardly swallow the pieces in front of me.

Julian talked to Mami and Abuelita about going to *el norte* someday.

And Mami sighed. "Not now," she said. "Not until you're taller than I am."

Abuelita winked at Julian. He was inches taller.

The next time I waded down the creek, I saw that the stones on the woman's path were back in place and swept clean.

And I was sure Julian had done that.

What had Abuelita said? Everyone has something. Julian had his painting. But much more than that.

chapter 18

moving

It's another morning; we're sitting at the kitchen table. Angel is bent over a page from the notebook, working in her loopy handwriting. And I'm asking for English words: *owl*, *bobcat*, and *deer*. And then: *gray rocks* and *cave*.

She draws in her breath at a noise outside. The rattling of an old truck? Is it coming down the alley?

She jumps up quickly, goes to the window, and lifts the curtain an inch or two.

"What?" I ask absently, gray rocks and the cave still on my mind.

She turns and I see she's afraid. She gives her head a quick shake, her fingers go to her lips.

I jump up and peer out. It really is a truck. The alley is narrow; the top of the truck grazes the trees, and leaves scatter. It stops directly behind the house.

Two men, both whistling, come around to open the back of the truck. It's hard to see what's inside, but Angel takes a guess. "Furniture," she says. "They're coming here. Someone's moving in."

She might be right. The men put their heads together to check a piece of paper and one of them points toward our kitchen.

But they don't come, not yet. They hop up and sit on the edge of the truck, with coffee cups in their hands. They're in no hurry.

But we are.

We move fast, scooping everything up from the table, the paper, the backpacks, the guitar against the wall. The ads we studied slide away onto the floor; the picture of the woman with the bracelets snaking up her arm stares up at me. I leave them there.

What else do we need?

We grab the food that Sal has given us, sweeping it out of the cabinet, and the money I've left on the counter.

I remember the flashlight on the couch and dive for it.

Do we have everything? I stare at the pile on the floor in front of us. How have we gotten all these things? I came here with almost nothing, and now there's really no way to carry it all.

Angel frowns. "We won't even get out the front door."

In spite of our rush to get somewhere safe before the men open the back door, I give Angel a quick grin and she nods.

There's no time to pick and choose. We leave half bottles of soda on the counter, and then we run out the front door with whatever we can carry, as we hear the back door open.

We're just in time. We're not caught.

We look around, hoping no one is on the street to see us in the daytime. A car passes, and we duck our heads, but it doesn't even slow down.

"Where, Matty?" Angel mumbles. "Where?" and I tell her, "We'll go to the pine forest."

"That's a terrible idea." She raises her hand without thinking and drops a can of food. It rolls down the street.

"Not so terrible." I go after it. "You'll see, Angel."

The cave and the gray rocks are still in my mind. I wish I knew how large that cave was. Suppose it isn't even a cave, but only a jagged bunch of rocks with nowhere to sit inside?

Still, we hurry down the street. The sun is hidden behind sullen gray clouds, and it's so hot it's hard to move.

We look over our shoulders; we have to run, we have to hide. I can't wait to reach the friendly arms of the pine trees.

We turn left, taking the straight road toward that cool place with the cave.

The trees are up ahead, that green fuzz that promises safety. I hitch up Sal's food, the guitar over my shoulder, and run the last few feet. I show Angel the sandy path, our feet scattering pine needles.

I'm in such a hurry that I take a wrong turn and the cave isn't in front of us. I can't even see gray rocks.

"I'm lost." I can hardly get the words out. "I can't find . . ."

I dump everything on the ground in front of me.

"Slow down," Angel says. "Take a few breaths. We'll be all right."

She doesn't mean it, though. I see her glance over her shoulder, even though I know the men unloading furniture are far behind us, and there's no one nearby.

I pick up our bundles, and we wander into grass that's high as our knees and bends gently in the hot wind. Underneath, the ground is soft, and the pine trees surround us with thick branches.

I feel safer here.

Angel still doesn't feel that. She zigzags ahead of me, dragging our things.

But then she slows down, stops, out of breath, and I catch up to her. We sit at the edge of the field. Around us, noise begins. It's the sound of frogs, so maybe we're close to a pond. One frog begins, *glunk, glunk,* another chimes in, and then a third. Over our heads a bird flies up. *"Talk to me, talk to me,"* it seems to say.

The sun comes out and plays over our eyes. We close them and yawn. We doze for a while, leaning against our bags.

But later, the wind is stronger, flattening the tall grass. The birds are silent, and only the frogs continue their strange music.

"We have to sleep somewhere tonight, really sleep," Angel says.

"Yes, you're right. You're always right," I say, trying to make her smile.

We leave our bags under a tree, careful to remember exactly where they are. Then we wander, and almost like a miracle, the trees and the narrow path begin to look familiar. "The cave is near."

She doesn't answer. She's fed up with the pines and the wind blowing through the grass.

Maybe she's even fed up with me.

We duck under trees, the guitar still slung over my back, and there in front of us is a jumble of stones, almost hidden behind trees with uneven arms and bent trunks.

I think of the bobcat, but I don't tell Angel that the cave might be too small for us, or even that an animal might be living there.

I switch on the flashlight. Its thin beam shines into a pair of dark eyes, a groundhog maybe, which lumbers away and disappears.

"Wait here a minute," I tell Angel.

She slides down against a bare tree and closes her eyes.

As terrible as all this is, I have to smile. I'm really in charge: the boss of the pine-tree world.

Not Angel.

She knows it. She's not happy about it.

We don't go into the cave yet. I'm glad to put it off, and I think Angel is too. We spread our things around us: the guitar, Sal's food, a can opener, bottles of water, of soda, spoons. . . .

"Where's . . . ?" I begin.

"What?"

"The quilt from the bed."

I don't say it's the quilt Mami and Abuelita worked on at our table in the kitchen, probably sewing while I stood at the stove taking spoonfuls of rice from the pot.

How could I have forgotten it? How could I leave it there for someone else?

It's the quilt they made for Julian.

"I'm going back for it."

She shakes her head, then changes her mind. "Yes, we'll need it."

She doesn't offer to come with me, and I'm glad. I have to do this alone.

chapter 19

the quilt

The truck is gone; no one is around. But still, I move slowly, looking everywhere to be sure I'm alone. I dart across the yard, empty houses on each side of me, and go up the three steps to the door.

It's locked now.

But maybe the kitchen window.

I give it a push and it creaks up, I boost myself to straddle the sill, and then I'm inside. If people saw me now they'd be sure I'm a thief.

I feel like one.

I slide into the bedroom, passing a living room with a different couch, striped, cleaner than the one that was here before, a couple of chairs, tables, and a bookcase that's filled with books.

I can't waste a moment. Whoever owns all this must be coming.

The quilt isn't in the bedroom. A pale blanket is spread across the bed. Have they taken Mami's away in the truck with the old couch? If only I had remembered to take it!

Back in the kitchen, I close the window. This time I go out the door.

There's a clean garbage can next to the bottom step. I open the lid. The picture of the lady with the bracelets looks up at me, and underneath . . .

Mami and Abuelita's red and yellow quilt!

I pull it out, careful to keep it off the ground, rolling it up. I hug it to me, almost as if Mami and Abuelita are there beside me, and Julian too.

And then I hurry back to the forest, to Angel, and the cave.

It isn't huge, it isn't even big, but it's enough for the two of us. At least, that's what I think at first.

We sit just inside under a rocky roof, wishing we'd taken the rest of the food we'd left in the cabinet; we listen to the plink of water dripping inside.

It's hot and humid, and the rocks are hard even with the quilt folded underneath us. In the distance I hear the roll of thunder. I think I've never felt worse.

"Remember that first soup?" Angel says.

I do. Then I sit up straight.

Sal.

"We can't stay here in this heat," Angel whispers, as if someone might hear us. She pulls her hair up off her neck. "It's worse than prison."

I stand up quickly and stumble over one of the bags. "I have to go back right away. Sal thinks I'm coming to help today."

I think of Miguel and the factory; I think of the fist-sized dent in the car door. I even think of taking the old woman's broom. I've done so many things wrong! But I can't let Sal down.

"Just stay here, Angel," I tell her. "I'll come back when I can. I'll give you the flashlight so you won't be alone in the dark later." I turn it on to show her.

She looks furious. "You think I'm going to stay here? When you come back, I might be gone."

"Gone again?" I don't say it nicely. At the same time I drop the flashlight. It rolls between us, lighting the floor of the cave, lighting . . .

Something familiar?

But there's no time to go back and look.

Angel's face is flushed from the heat, and I feel sorry

for her. "Listen. I'll come back as soon as I finish work. We'll figure something out."

She barely looks at me, but she nods, and then I crash through the trees. I'm a mess, with twigs in my hair, and my face probably filthy.

I run along the streets, past the houses, along the avenue.

How could I have forgotten?

There's a crack of lightning. I actually see it—an angry flash that zigzags across the sky, and a clap of thunder so loud it makes me jump.

But the store is in front of me. Kids are coming out of school, so I'm not late after all.

Inside, Sal is turned away from me, taking an order on the telephone, I guess.

I rush into the little bathroom in back that's filled with boxes and pails. I turn on the faucet and dunk my head in the sink to wet my hair, my face, and my neck. I wash with soap until my nails are clean. Then I shake the twigs out from the bottom of my shirt. I'm ready to work.

I get the broom and sweep around the front, thinking of Miguel at the factory. The car I dented wasn't his. Did he have to pay for it? Did he have to explain to the owner that two kids were playing ball with a piece of the motor?

I can't think about that now.

I sweep harder, then lean the broom against the back wall. Sal waves at a few cartons. I know exactly what to do. I rip open those cartons, pile cans of dog food on the dog food shelf, canned peas on the vegetable shelf, and root beer in the refrigerator.

There's another flash of lightning; I look up waiting for the thunder . . .

Which doesn't come.

Sal, at the counter now, wipes his hands on his apron. He's glancing out too.

"A storm," I say, one of my new words.

"No. Heat lightning." He makes sure I understand, raising his arm in a zigzag motion. "Zzzzz," he says.

"Yes. Lightning."

He talks slowly, still using his arms. "If the lightning hits a tree . . ." He stops and waits for me to catch up as I mouth the words.

"Boom!" he yells.

I jump.

"The tree explodes."

"Fire?" I ask, and he nods.

I think of the pine forest, and Angel sitting in the cave.

How soon until I go back? I look up at the clock.

Sal sees me watching. "Take some food, Matty." He points to the shelves. "Help yourself. Then go home. See you tomorrow?"

I nod. "See you tomorrow."

I take water, oranges, and juice, things to quench our thirst on this hot day; then I make two sandwiches, rye bread with ham and cheese and mayonnaise dripping out the sides.

Sal reaches out with money, but I shake my head. "Enough," I say, pleased that I know that word.

I rush back to Angel, glancing up at the sky. One cloud rolls over another and thunder rumbles in the distance.

chapter 20

the cave

We sit at the edge of the cave, the quilt under us, munching on Sal's sandwiches, not talking. We can't stay here. Tonight is all right, maybe even tomorrow, but this isn't a place to live.

I think of everything I've done to find Julian: walking along the street looking for him, climbing the building, asking the women at the factory, even hoping there'd be a clue in the house we've just left. I can't imagine one more place to search for him. And then I wonder: could I find that woman, Elena, and ask her?

Next to me, Angel slurps down water and peels back the orange rind.

"Matty?" she says.

From her voice, I know she's holding back tears. "I think about going back. Maybe I belong with my grandfather." She brushes her cheeks. "I dreamed last night that I was in school, that I could read and write, that my grandfather was waiting for me at the gate in the afternoon, asking if I had a good day."

"Was it a happy dream?"

"I don't know. The dream was over before I found out. But maybe I do have to find out. We could stay here, just another day. I'll keep learning words. But just a day, no more, even if I don't go home."

"We have to look for another place," I say.

"But if I did go home, I'd tell my grandfather I can't read. Maybe then he'd help."

She's really thinking about it. I imagine crossing the border again, that terrible trip, but worse this time because I have to tell Mami and Abuelita and even Lucas that I didn't find Julian, never even came close.

Don't think about it right this minute.

I put my empty water bottle back in Sal's bag. "Angel? I'm going to take a look in back of the cave." I stand as a bolt of lightning streaks across the sky, the light flashing from one end of the horizon to the other.

I take the flashlight. It really isn't much of a cave. As I go in, the wall slopes on each side, the ceiling slants downward with a thin line of water pooling in one corner. I have to duck my head to walk farther.

And then I see it! It's so small it would be easy to miss: a splash of paint, a river of blue, a hint of a boy standing at the edge.

I'm the boy.

Julian is the artist.

He's been here, right where I'm standing, and I feel how close he must be.

I put my fingers over the blue river, over the boy, and I hold back tears.

I go out to Angel. "I think you'll be happy in school," I say. "But maybe not yet. Maybe you'll wait a little longer, just until I find Julian. Because now I will. I know I will."

She stares up at the sky, and then at our poor things gathered around us. "I guess so."

So I take Mami's quilt—the home quilt, I call it in my mind—and spread it out inside. I bring in the rest of the things and put them under the painting. All we have to do is wait for the next few hours when it will be dark, and hope for rain that will cool off the rest of the world.

In the meantime, I tear off a piece of paper from Felipe's notebook, which Angel and I share now, and begin to write; it's just bits and pieces about what's happened to me since I've been here. I search for a word to say what it was like to see that painting, to know that Julian is nearby.

So I'm not going home.

I'm going to keep looking.

Tomorrow I'll find the woman who owns that ghost building and ask her about Julian. Sal might know where she lives.

I fill the paper in front of me now, half listening to Angel as she writes too, mumbling the words. I can hear the satisfaction in her voice.

But the air feels strange, the light in the sky almost a neon green. An animal crashes through the trees nearby. Are we really safe here in this rocky cave?

chapter 21

fire

The next bolt of lightning and the thunder that follows are so close that the ground seems to vibrate. There's another huge crack. It almost deafens me.

Angel jumps to her feet, her paper floating away from her, and takes three steps out of the cave.

I'm up too. I see a curl of smoke and a flash of fire bursting from the top of the highest tree nearby.

The tree explodes, sending showers of sparks up and out to cover the branches nearby.

I push Angel back into the cave, but she grabs my

arm. "We won't be able to breathe," she says. "We'll have to run."

I glance back at the quilt, at the guitar; they're lost. But that's only the moment before we run. Hands covering our heads, we rush down the narrow path, feeling the heat of the fire behind us, mouths open to the smoke, coughing. . . .

We throw ourselves down at the edge of the road, gasping for breath.

And I see . . .

A truck comes to a stop, almost hitting the nearest tree. Three people jump out. Angel and I scramble out of the way as they pull a huge round hose off the back and attach it to a fire hydrant I didn't notice.

They pass us, and I realize that one of them is Elena, who owns the ghost building.

I don't know who the second is. A man.

But the third . . .

The third person . . .

Brushes my head as he drags the hose, the water, coming now, gushing.

It's my brother.

Julian.

chapter 22

found

"Boys don't cry," Damian said once.

"He's wrong," Abuelita told me, her voice fierce. "Good men cry because they care."

I'm glad she said that, because I'm crying, really crying, now.

Angel thinks it's about the fire. "It wasn't your fault," she keeps saying, her hands on my shoulders. "And those people will put it out."

I can't answer. I stand there, not even trying to hide the tears. I grab her arm, shaking my head. I feel the tick of my heart, because I'm afraid now for Julian, and the other two, so close to the smoke and the fire.

Over the flaming trees, water sprays in a thick arc, back and forth. Several branches split and crash to the ground. The heat is so fierce that Angel and I move across the street where several people have gathered, watching, pointing. No one seems to wonder about who we are, or care; they move over to make room for us.

Flashes of lightning zigzag across the sky, one after another, and there's a constant rumble of thunder. But finally, I feel it . . .

Great drops of water on my head as rain comes at last.

I raise my face to it, open my mouth to drink it in, and watch as a few sparks continue to fly up, the flames lessen, and slowly, the fire dies.

My crying has stopped now, but not the rain. It comes down in torrents, bringing cool air.

The people scatter, and I know Julian will be coming back out soon. Did he see me as he went by? Or did he run his hand over the top of my head because I was just a kid standing there?

"All right now?" Angel says.

I nod and raise my hand toward the fire. "My brother Julian."

"Oh, Matty!" she says, finally realizing and almost

dancing around me. Her face changes, and I'm sure she's thinking about her grandfather, and maybe how glad she'll be to see him, to be home.

Now the three are dragging back the hose, and Julian stops, and of course he knows it's me.

In two steps, he's in front of me, his face filthy. He reaches out, his hands in thick gloves, and lifts me off the ground.

He's not crying the way I did; he's laughing, a wonderful sound as he swings me around the way I might swing Lucas in the kitchen.

Behind him is Elena, her head tilted. And Julian turns. "My brother! He's come to find me. My brother Mateo, the writer." There's a catch in his voice.

She smiles at me, her eyes bright blue in her soot-covered face. "Sal's boy."

They wind up the hose; then we ride back in the truck, all of us squeezed together. It's dark now, the headlights on, the windshield wipers sliding back and forth, and I don't know where we're going, but it doesn't make any difference.

We could drive forever.

chapter 23

elena

We sit in Elena's kitchen at a round wooden table until the sun comes up through the window.

We never stop talking, interrupting each other, telling our stories as Elena brings lemonade and donuts, and then, in the middle of the night, hot tea and toast with butter and cinnamon.

The kitchen walls are covered with paintings: one is of a garden with an overhanging tree, birds sitting on the branches. I know Julian has painted it. It's not hard to figure out, because under the tree, if you look carefully, you'll see a small house on the edge of a creek.

Our house.

Next to me, Angel smiles. She knows how happy I am. I've finally found Julian.

"When Tomàs left, I had to stay here," Julian says, "because I owed Elena money."

Elena doesn't understand Spanish; she looks from one of us to the other.

But I understand more than Spanish. I picture the money Tomàs put on our table. *The boss paid us a week ahead.*

"Like the miserable woman's broom," I whisper.

And Julian puts his hand on my shoulder. "Yes."

He tells us then about living in the cave because he thought he might be caught in the house, working at the terrible factory, and going back to Elena with the money at last.

He sweeps his hand around. "I painted Elena's kitchen." He grins. "I even put out fires in her forest."

He glances toward her, and she looks back and smiles. "Julian's been a big help."

I see how much they care about each other.

"But Mami," I say. "Abuelita. They don't know where you are."

"They must by now. I know the mail is slow at home, but I wrote to them. And I've been working. People have seen what I've done and asked me to paint for them. Soon, I'll be able to send money to the bank again."

He stands and takes the teapot from Elena. "I'm trying to apply for a green card. And one day, I'll become a citizen. Elena and her friends are studying the law. It may take a long time, but it's what I want more than anything."

I nod; his face is filled with hope.

But then I think of the quilt and the guitar in the cave, both gone.

Julian sees my face. "What's wrong?"

Even after this long night, Julian drives me back to the forest. There's a strong smell of smoke, and wisps of it float in the air. A patch of trees raising ghostly arms, twisted and bare without their branches. The pine needles underneath are black as licorice.

But the things we left in the cave are safe: Sal's food, the bottles and cans still fine. And so is Lucas's guitar, under the painting in the back of the cave. Mami's quilt is darker and needs washing, but I fold it, holding it up to my face. And Julian runs his hands over it.

We find a place to sit. "How brave you've been," Julian tells me.

Is that true? I'm reminded of Abuelita, who was sure I could find him. Maybe I was stronger than I thought I'd be.

I look across at him, my brother, my friend. How hard it will be to go back home without him.

"Do me a favor?" he asks.

"Sure."

He pulls a pad out of his pocket. "Bring this home for me?"

I open the small book. It's filled with drawings of Texas and Arkansas. There are sketches of Mami holding Lucas as a baby, and several of me writing at the kitchen table. On the last page, he's painted a picture of Abuelita: she's young, her braid is dark, and her face is unlined.

"Abuelita, the heart of our family." He taps the book.

"'Everyone has something,' Abuelita told me. 'And, Julian, you will be a fine painter.'"

He touches the book. "I hope that will be true."

I nod, because it's too hard to speak. Abuelita, who wants something for both of us, and Lucas, who will be the musician in the family.

We sit there for a few minutes longer. It may be a long time before we're together again.

He throws his arm around me for that last second. And then we take everything back to Elena's. There's enough room for all of us to sleep, and that's what I do, the small book tucked away in my pocket.

last day

I walk to Sal's and tell him I've found my brother and I'm going home.

"Wonderful!" He tilts his head. "I'll miss you, though."

I nod, then sweep the back and the front, even in the corner. I make sure there's no dust in the cabinets. I unpack the few cartons that are piled up near the door and put the canned food on the shelves.

And then it's time to leave.

Sal throws his arms around me. "You're a good guy, Matty. Anyone will give you a job."

I think of Miguel. "I hope so."

Sal hands me a bag he's filled with marshmallow cookies and bottles of water. There are cans of fruit swimming in juice, and small packages of peanuts.

"Everything you'll need for your trip, I hope," he says.

He gives me money, too. Maybe I shouldn't take it, but I know I'll need it. "Thank you," I say. I realize I've understood every word, and answered exactly right.

Well, almost.

Sal is chewing his mustache, trying not to smile, so I tell him goodbye in Spanish. "I'll write a letter to you someday, and send you my first book." He doesn't understand that, of course. It's hard to speak more than one language.

By the time I head back to Elena's house, it's almost night and she's cooking a special dinner. I hurry, thinking about what I'll say to Angel.

She's sitting on a bench in the sweet-smelling garden. I slide in next to her. "It's time to go home," I say.

She nods. "Home." I can hear how much she wants it.

"You'll see your grandfather. You'll be able to go to school now. We'll cross the border together."

She stares at Elena's flowers; then I hear the sound of her wonderful laugh. "You can't cross the border alone? You can't even do that by yourself?"

I grin too. "I guess not."

"I'll have to do it, then. You'll get lost by yourself."

She roots around in the bag from Sal and opens the cookies.

We talk through dinner. I tell Julian about Lucas and his music; I tell him that a cat hangs around and I might give her a name. I tell him about Miguel and that I'm determined to get my job back.

He talks about his painting. He wants the world to know about our country, and so every piece he does has something of us.

Later, I put my few things in a backpack, and then Julian and I walk to the forest in the dark. It's windy tonight, and the sharp, piney smell is in the air. I breathe it in, watching the doe as she lies under the trees, almost covered. I think she might be having her fawn, but I won't be here to see it. I won't see the bobcat that hissed at me, or the groundhog that lumbers along the paths.

It's really late now, and I'm tired. I run my fingers through the branches, feeling the soft green needles in my hands, and snap off a small twig to take home with me.

"Goodbye, forest," I say aloud without thinking, and Julian rests his hand on my shoulder. The deer doesn't move, and I back away, not wanting to disturb her.

At Elena's house, I curl up on the couch.

Last time.

chapter 25

going home

Julian calls Felipe to say that we're coming, and then he and Elena put us on the bus to Samson, a long trip. When we get off, our water is gone, and most of Sal's food and the lunch Elena packed for us. But Felipe is waiting for us at the station, and takes us home, ready to fill us with bacon and eggs. He grins at us. "You're lucky. Friends of mine are driving south tomorrow and will take you with them. It will be an easier trip this time."

We follow him into the kitchen and can hardly wait as he fries up eggs for us.

"I'm ready to go home," I say as we shovel in the food.

Angel and I smile at each other. "It's easier going south than north," she says. "We belong there, after all."

I want to tell Angel I'll miss her, but she knows.

After we eat, we memorize addresses. Her grandfather's place is hours away from mine. A small distance for travelers like us.

She puts her hand on my shoulder. "Now that I know where you live, look for me. You'll see me one day."

"I will," I say, and I really will. "I'll never forget you, Angel."

She reaches out to hug me, not saying a word. I hug her too, Angel, my best friend.

The crossing and the desert are ahead of us, but I'm not afraid. And then I'll be taking the train with Felipe's friends.

Angel and I say a last goodbye in the car. Soon I'll go down Creek Road, the slow-moving water at my side, the trees over my head. I'll see my sky-blue house, and Julian's painting on every wall. The cat will come to greet me, its sharp claws on my legs.

I'll open the door. "Is anyone here?" I'll call, then they'll surround me, Mami and Abuelita, Lucas yelling "Mateo!" as I put the guitar in his hands.

We'll sit at the table and look at Julian's drawings. They'll all be crying. I suppose I'll be crying too, but the tears will be mostly happy.

I'll go into the bedroom I share with Lucas and put the sprig of pine on the table between us.

Later, I'll go to the factory. I'll tell Miguel how sorry I am about the car. I'll ask him to give me one more chance. "I'm a good worker now." I think he'll say yes.

But there's one more thing. I'll write about what has happened, the north and the south, and Julian, and Angel.

Someday.

From the first novel of Mateo Cortez

Until I Find Julian

My eyes are closing as I listen to the sound of the motor and try to breathe in that close dark air. I'm almost asleep.

Dreaming, Mateo. That's it. I'm lost in dreams.

I see our house, which tilts against the creek; it's miles behind me, weeks behind me. I hear Abuelita's voice as she reads to me. My little brother, Lucas, dances around the kitchen. Beans simmer on the stove. Oh, and Mami's arms fold themselves around me. . . .

about the author

Patricia Reilly Giff is the author of many beloved books for children, including the Kids of the Polk Street School books, the Friends and Amigos books, and the Polka Dot Private Eye books. Several of her novels for older readers have been chosen as ALA-ALSC Notable Children's Books and ALA-YALSA Best Books for Young Adults. They include *The Gift of the Pirate Queen; All the Way Home; Water Street; Nory Ryan's Song*, a Society of Children's Book Writers and Illustrators Golden Kite Honor Book for Fiction; and the Newbery Honor Books *Lily's Crossing* and *Pictures of Hollis Woods. Lily's Crossing* was also chosen as a *Boston Globe–Horn Book* Honor Book. Her most recent books are *Winter Sky,*

Gingersnap, R My Name Is Rachel, Storyteller, Wild Girl, and *Eleven,* as well as the Zigzag Kids series. She lives in Connecticut.

Patricia Reilly Giff is available for select speaking engagements. To inquire about a possible appearance, please contact the Penguin Random House Speakers Bureau at speakers@penguinrandomhouse.com.